D1114910

ALSO BY CLAUDIA MILLS

Dinah Forever
Losers, Inc.
Standing Up to Mr. O.
You're a Brave Man, Julius Zimmerman
Lizzie at Last
7 × 9 = Trouble!
Alex Ryan, Stop That!
Perfectly Chelsea
Makeovers by Marcia
Trading Places
Being Teddy Roosevelt
The Totally Made-up Civil War Diary of Amanda MacLeish
How Oliver Olson Changed the World

ONE
SQUARE
INCH

ONE SQUARE INCH

Claudia Mills

FARRAR STRAUS GIROUX
New York

www.fsgkidsbooks.com

Library of Congress Cataloging-in-Publication Data
Mills, Claudia.
    One square inch / Claudia Mills.— 1st ed.
        p.   cm.
    Summary: When their mother's behavior changes and she starts
to neglect them, seventh-grader Cooper and his little sister take
refuge in Inchland, an imaginary country inspired by deeds to one
square inch of land that their grandfather gave them.
    ISBN: 978-0-374-35652-1 (alk. paper)
    [1. Mothers—Fiction.   2. Brothers and sisters—Fiction.
3. Family problems—Fiction.   4. Imagination—Fiction.]
I. Title.

PZ7.M63963Oq 2010
[Fic]—dc22
                                                          2009037287

To Rachel Sailer,
who listens always

ONE
SQUARE
INCH

1

Sometimes magic turns up in unexpected places. Not real magic, if there is such a thing, which my younger sister, Carly, still believes in but I don't, at least not anymore. But magic that you can sort of pretend to believe in. Magic that is real enough, and sometimes realer than anything else in your life. Looking back, I think it's strange that it was Gran-Dan of all people who first gave Carly and me the deeds to Inchland.

We were visiting him in New Jersey, Carly, my mom, and me. Our family is just the three of us, so we did everything together: my dad was killed in a car accident when I was only four and Carly had just been born. I don't know if I have any memories of my dad, or if I just think I do because other people have told me stories about him.

Anyway, we were in New Jersey, and it was hot, hot, hot, so much hotter than it ever seems to get in Colorado, and Carly and I were playing pirates on Gran-Dan's wide back porch, which I have to say made a great deck of a pirate ship. I was the pirate king, of course. Betrayed by my own men, gravely wounded, weakened by loss of blood, I turned to face the enemy. "Die, you mangy dog!" I shouted, brandishing my fearsome sword.

"No, *you* die," the enemy retorted.

The pirate king's blade slashed through the air. "Die, I said!"

"I can't die!" The enemy's voice rose higher. "I can't die *now*, Cooper. I have to go to the bathroom."

"Aw, Carly." I shoved my cardboard sword back into its cardboard scabbard. "You always have to go to the bathroom right when you're about to be stabbed."

"But I do have to go."

"Well, go then."

Carly flashed me a relieved smile. Off she ran, her bobbing blond pigtails making her look more like a seven-year-old than a bloodthirsty pirate. The beanbag parrot she had taped onto her shoulder fell off as she disappeared into the house. I followed after her and picked it up.

"Pieces of eight," I made the parrot squawk.

"Aw, pipe down," I said to the parrot.

Hot and sweaty now, I plopped onto a worn wooden chair by Gran-Dan's kitchen table and looked out the window into his huge shaded yard. There were so many more trees of all kinds in New Jersey than in Colorado. The yard was full of great places to make a secret fort or castle or pirate lair.

I lifted my damp hair off my forehead. It was hard to get used to the warm, sticky air.

A cool glass of lemonade might help. Just as I was pouring it, Gran-Dan appeared beside me. I gulped down half the glass in two swallows.

"You're drinking too fast, you'll get a stomach cramp," he said.

That was what Gran-Ellen always used to say, but I've never had a stomach cramp and never heard of anyone getting one, except in Gran-Ellen's warnings about drinking cold liquids too quickly on a hot day. She always used to say it like she was really concerned about how terrible a stomach cramp would be if we actually got one. For Gran-Dan, it was one more thing he could be critical about.

"Where's your mother?" he asked. "I haven't seen her yet this morning."

The question irritated me. Gran-Dan had to know that my mom was still sleeping. It wasn't *that* late, maybe ten o'clock, maybe ten-thirty. Counting the two-hour time change, it wasn't late at all. Besides, lots of people slept longer when they were on vacation.

"I think she's still asleep," I said.

Gran-Dan looked at his watch. "At quarter till eleven? What grown adult sleeps until noon like a teenager?"

Before I could answer, Carly came back into the kitchen. Gran-Dan's eyes lit up at the sight of her. It was okay with me, I guess, that he liked her best.

"Ahoy, matey," he said by way of greeting. "How's the pirate business?"

Carly giggled. "Cooper was about to stab me to death, but then I had to go to the bathroom."

Gran-Dan chuckled. I knew he thought it was silly that an eleven-year-old boy would still be playing pirates, but I only did it for Carly. Well, mostly for Carly. If my mom had been feeling better, she would have been in the game, too, as the pirate queen, and Gran-Dan would have thought that was even worse.

"Where's your mother?" Gran-Dan asked Carly. Apparently, it wasn't enough that he'd already asked me, and that I had already told him.

"Sleeping," Carly said.

Gran-Dan checked his watch again.

"She loves to sleep," Carly said.

Gran-Dan gave a snort of disapproval.

Fortunately, I heard soft footsteps on the stairs. My mom was finally up, though still in her bathrobe, her reddish curls uncombed.

"Good *morning*," Gran-Dan said. The "morning" was obviously sarcastic. Then he asked, in a kinder voice, "Are you feeling all right?" For Gran-Dan, the only possible excuse for sleeping so late would be if you were sick, preferably dying.

"I'm just tired, that's all," Mom said.

"The best thing when you're tired isn't excess sleep, it's exercise," Gran-Dan announced. "If I'm tired, I take a brisk walk, or a bike ride, and it does the trick every time."

Well, maybe everybody in the world wasn't like Gran-Dan. But I wasn't going to say it.

"When was the last time you had a checkup?" It was clear that Gran-Dan wasn't going to let this thing go. "You might have mono. Remember that girl in your class who had mono in high school? If you're that tired, you should be having a checkup."

There was an awkward silence.

"Well," Gran-Dan said with fake heartiness. "We're going into New York tomorrow, and down the shore on Tuesday, but what are the plans for this afternoon? We may be getting a late start, but that's no reason to waste the whole day."

"Stay here and play?" Carly said. I was grateful Carly had said it first, not me.

"Come on, you two can play any time. This is your chance to do some sightseeing. What about Morristown? See Washington's headquarters during the Revolutionary War? Cooper, you must have studied that in school last year. Schools still teach some history these days, don't they?"

The thought of walking around looking at old Revolutionary War cannons in the 97-degree heat had zero appeal to me.

"We just got here yesterday," I said, hoping Gran-Dan would think that was a reason to laze around doing nothing, or what he would think of as doing nothing.

"Emily?" Gran-Dan asked my mom.

"Staying here is fine with me." She didn't look up from untying and retying the belt on her robe.

Gran-Dan shrugged. "That's settled then," he said. If he was disappointed, at least he didn't say it.

Carly blew upward at her bangs. "It's hot today."

"It's cooler down in the basement," Gran-Dan suggested. If I had said anything about the heat, Gran-Dan would have said, "Complaining won't make it any cooler." The only thing Gran-Dan hated more than sleeping late was complaining about anything, unless Carly was the one doing the complaining.

Gran-Dan's house wasn't air-conditioned—he didn't believe in air-conditioning—but he tried to keep the house cool with drawn drapes and ceiling fans. It wasn't very cool right now.

"We could play being Eskimos!" Carly said. "We could make an igloo out of . . . What could we use to make an igloo, Cooper?"

I wasn't exactly an expert on igloo building, but I tried to think. Big blocks of ice and snow. Styrofoam might be good.

"Do you have any big blocks of Styrofoam?" I asked Gran-Dan.

"I imagine I could find some."

He led Carly and me down to a corner of the dark basement piled high with boxes stacked on the bare concrete floor; he must have had the boxes for everything he had bought in the last forty years.

"A lot of these cartons have Styrofoam inserts," he said. "Use whatever you want, but make sure you put everything back where you found it."

Gran-Dan's house was completely neat and organized, ever since Gran-Ellen died three years ago. She and my mom were the two creative, messy ones; Gran-Dan was the one who liked order and neatness and everything in its place. I liked order and neatness, too, but I couldn't see keeping dozens of Styrofoam inserts, each one tucked carefully into its original box.

I was glad when Gran-Dan went upstairs and left Carly and me alone to start building.

An hour later, we had a large, if somewhat lopsided, Styrofoam igloo. I did most of the construction work, but I like building things. Carly had run upstairs and found some of our mom's old dolls and was putting them to bed inside the igloo's snug walls. Carefully, she bundled them up against the Arctic blizzard about to strike with its blinding snow and hundred-mile-an-hour winds.

"Lunchtime!" Gran-Dan called.

We left our igloo behind and hurried up to the dining room. Gran-Dan didn't like to be kept waiting.

Lunch was tuna salad sandwiches and pickles and potato chips. I ate every bite on my plate so that Gran-Dan wouldn't tell me for the fiftieth time how when he was a boy he always ate every bite on his plate. I noticed that my mom ate every bite, too, for a change. She looked better now that she had gotten dressed, in shorts and a cheery pink top.

"Did you get your igloo built?" Gran-Dan asked Carly.

"Cooper made it. It's the best igloo in the whole world. I want to live in it forever! Can we sleep in it tonight? Can we?"

Gran-Dan didn't answer. I couldn't see any reason for him to object, but it looked like he was thinking about something else.

"Wait a minute," he said. "I just remembered something."

He left the table and was gone for a long time. I wanted to get up and go back to our nice, cool igloo, but I knew we were supposed to wait where we were.

When he finally returned to the table, he had something in his hand.

"Carly," he announced solemnly, "I have something to show you." He held out a sheaf of yellowed papers held together by a rusted paper clip.

"What are they?" Carly asked.

Gran-Dan paused for effect before answering. "These are the deeds to my land in the Yukon that I've had since I was ten years old. Each one is for one square inch of land up there in the snowy wilds of Canada where Sergeant Preston and his huskies used to roam. They're from a radio show back in the 1950s."

"Are they really deeds to real land?" I asked. "How did you get them?"

"By eating Quaker oats. One deed came in each box. That's all I wanted to do that winter, listen to Sergeant Preston on the radio and eat Quaker oats as fast as

I could, so I could get another deed to another square inch."

It was hard to imagine Gran-Dan as a boy, sprawled on the rug, listening to the radio, dreaming of faraway places.

My mom reached out her hand. "You never told me about them," she said to Gran-Dan.

Gran-Dan handed the deeds to Mom. "I forgot all about them until now."

"Can we have the deeds?" Carly begged. "Cooper and me?"

"How many are there?" Gran-Dan asked.

Carly took the deeds from Mom and counted them. "Eight."

"That makes four for each of you." I was surprised that he hadn't just given them all to Carly, though I know she would have shared with me; Carly and I always share everything.

Carly counted out four deeds for me and four for herself. Leaving them behind on the dining room table, she jumped up. "Come see our igloo! Come see it!"

"Let's just clear away our lunch things first," Gran-Dan said.

Carly's face fell.

"I'll take care of cleaning up," Mom offered.

I stayed behind to help while Gran-Dan followed Carly to the basement. To Carly, he'd probably praise the igloo to the skies; to me, he'd find some fault in how I had built it, or in the extra Styrofoam pieces I had left lying on the floor and forgotten to put away. I carried the plates into Gran-Dan's big, tidy kitchen and set them on the counter by the sink. Gran-Dan didn't have a dishwasher. He didn't believe in dishwashers, either.

When I returned to the dining room for the glasses, Mom was lingering at the table, looking at Gran-Dan's deeds.

"One square inch," she said. "A whole miniature world. All there in a box of cereal."

She handed my deeds to me. "Make sure you don't lose them," she said. "Though I know you won't."

That was the beginning of what was going to be Inchland. But I didn't know it then.

2

It rained the next morning, and we talked Gran-Dan out of taking the bus into New York City. My mom had always been the one who was eager to go into the city to see the shows at the Metropolitan Museum of Art or the Museum of Modern Art, but this time she said she was too tired to go. Right away Carly and I said we didn't want to go, either.

To my surprise, Gran-Dan actually looked relieved. "Well, it's five dollars each way just for the bus," he said. "And the older I get, the less I feel like fighting the crowds."

So Carly and I spent most of the day reading in our basement igloo. I had robbed our beds for a heap of pillows and blankets for padding against the scratchy Styrofoam walls. With a stack of books, one of Gran-Dan's flashlights, and a plate of cookies, I could have been content there forever.

But after I read the first chapter of one of Gran-Dan's old Freddy the Pig books, I started thinking about my mom. She had gone upstairs to bed right after supper last night, and I could tell that Gran-Dan was worried. Carly and I had almost gotten used to it—how, for the past two months, she slept late and napped during the day and then went to bed early and didn't have energy for anything anymore. But Gran-Dan hadn't seen her since Christmas.

"Do you hear the wind howling, Cooper?" Carly asked.

"Uh-huh," I said, even though the basement was utterly still and silent except for the occasional sound of one of us turning a page.

"How deep do you think it's going to snow?"

"Three feet?"

"Maybe four!" Carly beamed. She burrowed down into her nest of blankets and kept on reading.

I closed my book, saving my place with an old spelling test of Gran-Dan's that was tucked inside it. Gran-Dan was "Danny" back then. It was easier to imagine "Danny" collecting deeds to one square inch of the Yukon than grownup Gran-Dan.

Maybe my mom did have mono, like that person in her high school. The only thing I knew about mono was that it was called "the kissing disease." As far as I knew, my mom never kissed anybody, except for me and Carly, and that wasn't the kind of kissing that mattered. But if she did have mono, it would probably be all right. When Gran-Dan mentioned the girl who had it in high school, he hadn't said that she *died*.

Maybe it wasn't mono. What if she had cancer? She didn't smoke, and she always wore sunblock when she worked outside in the garden—when she used to work outside in the garden—but sometimes people just got cancer, for no reason at all.

"Where are you going?" Carly asked as I started crawling toward the igloo door.

"I'm going out to check on our pet seal, Selkie. To make sure she's doing all right in the blizzard."

"Okay," Carly said. "See if Gran-Dan will let us have any more cookies."

"Sure." I took the empty cookie plate and exited the igloo.

Upstairs, I turned on the computer on Gran-Dan's desk in the den. It was old and super slow, but I waited patiently for it to connect with the Internet. Then I Googled "seven warning signs of cancer." I had read about them once in a magazine but had forgotten them all, except for "obvious change in a wart or mole." I have this little brown mole on one shoulder, and sometimes it seems like it's growing bigger by the minute, but most of the time it seems like it's the same size that it's always been.

The list came up on the screen:

1. A change in bowel or bladder habits
2. A sore that does not heal
3. Unusual bleeding or discharge
4. Thickening or lump in the breast or elsewhere

5. Indigestion or difficulty in swallowing

6. Obvious change in a wart or mole

7. Nagging cough or hoarseness

None of the signs said anything about sleeping all the time. As far as I could tell, my mom didn't have any of the seven signs. I had "a sore that does not heal" from when I scraped my knee last month in a bike accident, but I knew the only reason it wasn't healing was that I kept picking the scab off.

I puffed out a long sigh of relief. From the list on the computer, it looked like my mom didn't have cancer after all.

When I returned to the igloo, Carly said, "So?"

"So?"

"Is she okay?"

"Mom?" How could Carly have known what I was doing?

"No! Selkie! Our pet seal!"

"Oh, sure. She likes when it snows. The more it snows, the happier seals get."

"What about the cookies?"

I had forgotten to ask.

"Well, it's pretty close to supper," Carly answered for me.

I took my place on my pile of pillows. I picked up my book but didn't open it. Instead I just gazed at the Styrofoam walls of the igloo, safe, for now, from the storm.

★ ★ ★

That evening the rain stopped, and Carly and I sat out-side on the steps of the big, screened back porch, waiting for the first fireflies. Fireflies were the best part of com-ing to New Jersey in the summer.

"Why don't we have fireflies in Colorado?" Carly asked.

"I don't know." I thought for a minute. "It's too dry, I guess."

"I see one!" Carly cried.

I followed her pointing finger. I didn't see anything. Then, in the dark mass of the hydrangea bushes at the edge of the lawn, one little light flickered.

"There's another one!" Carly left the porch and skipped across the wet grass to where the second firefly had signaled.

Which firefly decided to light up first? I wondered. The bravest? The most impatient? The one who was most eager to shine? If our family was fireflies, Carly would light up first. These days Mom probably wouldn't light up at all, but it wasn't that long ago when she would have been lighting up right along with Carly.

"Cooper, come!" Carly called. Unable to wait, she dashed back to the porch, holding her carefully cupped hands out in front of her. "I caught one!"

Crouching beside me, she opened her hands just enough that I could see the little pulse of light on the back of the bug. On, off, on again. It was funny that Carly, who was frightened of most bugs, wasn't afraid of fireflies.

She raced to the bushes to let the first firefly go and catch another. This one looked exactly like the last one, and I knew the third firefly would look the same. Still, I had to admit that it was magical to see that little light shining in her hand.

Now the bushes were all a-twinkle with fireflies, hundreds of them, thousands, like Christmas in August.

"Cooper, come!" Carly called again.

"I'll be there in a minute."

I slipped inside and went to Gran-Dan's computer. I could hear Mom talking with Gran-Dan in the living room; then I heard Gran-Dan's laughter. Feeling a bit foolish—Gran-Dan wouldn't be laughing like that if something was really wrong—I typed in "sleeps too much." A bunch of articles came up. I clicked on one and scanned the first couple of lines: the article said it was bad to sleep too much, even worse than sleeping not enough. I read a bit more: "Sleeping too much can lead to early death."

That couldn't be right. Nobody died just from *sleeping*. My mom was always telling me that I needed my sleep; I had never heard anyone say that there was anything wrong with sleeping. Well, except for Gran-Dan.

The article had to be wrong. My teacher last year in fifth grade kept telling us that we shouldn't believe everything we read on the Internet.

I shut down the computer and went outside. Carly was still in the yard, by the thicket of hydrangeas, busy catching and releasing one firefly after another.

"Do you think it's better to be a star or to be a fire-fly?" Carly asked.

It was one of the stranger questions I had ever heard. "Why?"

"I want to write a story about fireflies, and it's either going to be called *The Star That Wanted to Be a Firefly* or *The Firefly That Wanted to Be a Star.* Which do you think sounds better?"

"I think a firefly is more likely to want to be a star than a star is to want to be a firefly." That is, if a star could want to be anything at all. "I mean, we can see stars, but they can't see us."

"Okay," Carly said. "I'll write *The Firefly That Wanted to Be a Star.*"

"How is it going to end?"

"She ends up being happy that she's a firefly."

I caught a firefly on my first try. The fireflies didn't seem to mind being caught. On and off they blinked their little lights, whether they were free in the bushes or trapped within my fingers. Maybe they were too dumb to know the difference. Or maybe the difference didn't matter to them. Carly was right: they seemed pretty content being fireflies.

"Kids!" Gran-Dan called from the porch, his voice impatient. "Come in now. Time for baths and bed."

I opened my hands. And my firefly flitted away.

3

School began in late August: second grade for Carly, sixth grade—middle school!—for me. Usually every year my mom would complain that it was ridiculous for school to begin in August, that when she was growing up in New Jersey, school didn't start until after Labor Day. This year she didn't say anything. I thought she seemed even more sad and tired since our trip to New Jersey, but I tried not to think about it.

When we went shopping for school supplies, my mom hardly paid attention to what we bought. I was the one who had to help Carly read from her school supply list. "Five spiral-bound notebooks, wide-ruled," I told her.

Off she flew down the aisle, returning a minute later with an armful of notebooks. "I got one in each color—red, blue, green, yellow, purple. I like purple the best, but it would be confusing to have all purple, don't you think? I'll use purple for language arts, because I like language arts the best."

"What's next on the list?" I asked, since Mom didn't say anything. "One box of markers, wide-tipped, and one box of markers, narrow-tipped," I read.

Carly ran off to the marker display to retrieve them.

"Don't we have hundreds of markers at home?" Mom asked. She had never complained about buying new markers before.

"Most of them are dried-up," I said. Besides, everyone likes to have brand-new markers for the first day of school.

Mom turned away. When she took us shopping for school supplies last year, we came home with all kinds of things not on the list: miniature staplers, boxes of pastel chalks, index cards in every color of the rainbow.

"One box of twenty-four colored pencils," I told Carly after she put the markers in the cart.

"I love colored pencils!" Carly said.

Even though it was dumb to be so happy about a box of twenty-four colored pencils, I loved colored pencils, too.

Finally Carly's list was completed, and it was my turn. My list had some different items on it for middle school: two big three-ring binders, one for my morning classes and one for my afternoon classes; and three combination locks, one for my regular locker, one for my band locker, and one for my P.E. locker.

"Do you know how to work them?" Carly asked.

"I can figure it out," I said. I'd practice once we got home.

The total came to $98.17. Mom paid with her credit card. She didn't say anything about its being almost a hundred dollars, even though I knew she didn't earn very much, working at home as a graphic designer while trying to find time for her own collage making and quilting. Plus, she had to be earning less money lately: certainly she wasn't earning money while she was lying in bed sleeping.

"Second grade is going to be the best school year ever!" Carly said.

I grinned; it wasn't like Carly had much to compare it to. But she was probably right. Every year would be the best year for someone like Carly. And, who knew? Maybe sixth grade would be the best school year ever for me, too.

On the first day of school, Carly was so excited about second grade that she could hardly sit still during breakfast. I couldn't imagine liking school that much. Mom got up early enough to tie bright red ribbons on Carly's pigtails and then walked her the few blocks to Deer Creek Elementary. Western Hills Middle School started half an hour later than the elementary school and was farther away. On most days, I would take a public bus to and from school, but Mom told me she'd drive me there today, when she got home from walking Carly.

"Are you nervous about middle school?" she asked as she backed out of the driveway.

"Not really." I'm pretty good at finding my way around new places, and I had already mastered my three combination locks.

"Changing classes, having a locker, meeting new kids from other elementary schools?"

"It'll be okay."

But because I was grateful that she was taking an interest in something, I added, "Everyone says that Food Fun is a cool class."

She didn't say anything else until we pulled into the circle in front of Western Hills, where parents were dropping off their kids.

"I love you, Cooper," she said. She didn't usually say it, because she knew gushy things embarrassed me.

"I love you, too, Mom," I mumbled as I got out of the car. Then I relented and shot her a quick, encouraging grin.

On the blacktop outside school, I found my two best friends, Spencer and Ben. Spencer is short and chubby, negative about everything in a funny way. Ben is tall and athletic, almost embarrassed about how good he is at sports, schoolwork, and video games. I'm not sure how I fit into the trio. I'm not a comedian like Spencer, or perfect like Ben. I guess I'm the artistic one, who likes to paint and draw and make up stories, even though I never write them down. And I'm good with my hands, good at making things and building things and fixing things. The three of us have been friends since we were Carly's age.

"What do you have first period?" Ben asked.

I looked at my schedule. "Math."

"I have math, too—maybe we're in the same class."

"But you're in accelerated math, right?"

Ben's face fell. "Oh. Yeah. What do you have, Spence?"

"P.E. With Poached Egg."

I must have looked confused, because Spencer explained: "Coach Gregg."

Ben and I both laughed.

"I heard Poached Egg makes you do push-ups if you're late getting dressed," Spencer continued. With three older brothers, Spencer always heard lots of things. "I can't do push-ups. Not even one. So I'm going to have to get changed super fast. I think I'll wear my P.E. clothes under my regular clothes. Or maybe I'll get my mother to put Velcro on my clothes so I can just rip them off."

Ben and I laughed again.

The bell rang. The three of us joined the surging throng of sixth, seventh, and eighth graders streaming in through the main doors of the middle school.

Spencer and I had lockers close together; Ben's was down the hall by the gym. I got my lock opened right away. Four lockers down from me, Spencer was struggling.

"Fourteen. Thirty-seven. Eleven. Ta-da! Nope. Okay, try it again. Fourteen. Thirty-seven. Eleven. Ta-da! Nope. Open, you stupid lock! Open!"

I came over and gave it a try. The lock sprang open on my first attempt.

"How did you *do* that?" Spencer marveled.

I shrugged.

"My lock hates me," Spencer said. He stashed his afternoon binder in his locker and followed me down the hall. Then he peeled off to go to the gym while I took the stairs to the second floor for my first-period math class.

The math teacher, Miss Bellamy, seemed all right, though a bit too cheery for the first class of the morning. Her goal, she said, was to make everybody in the class love math! Because she loved math! And she loved teaching math! And she wanted all of her students, whatever their level of mathematical ability, to love math, too!

Good luck, I thought.

My second-period language arts teacher was the opposite. Mrs. Alpert didn't come right out and say that she wanted all her students to hate language arts, but she made it seem as if she would do everything in her power to make sure that we did. The worst crime we could ever commit, I gathered, was not to put our names in the *upper left corner* of the page. The second worst crime was to make a mistake in spelling *there, their,* and *they're.* If Mrs. Alpert had her way, that particular crime would be punishable by death.

From language arts I went to Food Fun, where I had both Spencer and Ben in my class. We would have one semester of Food Fun and then one semester of computer tech. The Food Fun teacher, Mr. Costa, was a large, young, jolly man with a booming voice. He loved to cook—and to eat—the way Miss Bellamy loved to solve math problems.

"By the end of September, all of you will be able to cook a tasty, nutritious meal for your families—*and* to wash the dishes afterward. By October, you'll be able to cook a company dinner for your relatives, and Aunt Agatha will be asking you for your recipes."

That sounded good to me. Meals at our house had been getting progressively worse since Mom had been sick, or whatever she was. These days we ordered a lot of pizza and take-out Chinese food. I didn't think I could ever get tired of pizza, but I was tired of it now.

"In November, we'll take a turn providing dinner for the hungry and homeless at a local church. In December, we'll put on a cooking show for the Western Hills Middle School community—'Costa Live.' And if any of you want to challenge me to a cook-off, I'll be ready. Have I missed any of the highlights? Oh, and we'll do a bake sale fund-raiser for the Western Hills music programs. Questions?"

Spencer raised his hand. "Will we do any cooking for *us*?"

Mr. Costa grinned. "Don't worry, we'll eat everything we cook here. Tell your parents you won't need lunch money this fall."

Fourth period I had P.E.; fifth period was lunch;

sixth period was band. Seventh period was science, with a substitute teacher, as the regular science teacher was on maternity leave; eighth period was social studies with Mr. Stuart, who wasn't funny but was soft-spoken and kind. Except for my crabby, strict L.A. teacher, all my teachers seemed friendly, especially Mr. Stuart and Mr. Costa, or Mr. Pasta, as Spencer had already nicknamed him.

After the final bell rang, Spencer still couldn't get his lock opened, so I did it for him again.

"Maybe there's a curse on it," Spencer suggested.

"Maybe there's a curse on *you*," I joked.

Two girls with lockers nearby were also struggling with their locks. "Cooper can do it," Spencer volunteered. "He's a combination lock genius."

The girls turned pleading eyes toward me. Embarrassed, but flattered, too, I walked over to them. "I can try," I said.

The first girl's lock opened for me as easily as Spencer's had, but the second girl's lock refused to open, even after three attempts.

"Are you sure you have the right combination?" I asked her.

"Yes! Twenty, eleven, sixteen." She fumbled in the bottom of her backpack for the piece of paper with her combination on it. "See? Oh, wait, it's twenty, *seven*, sixteen."

I twisted the dial, with the correct combination this time, and the lock sprang open.

"I told you he was a combination lock genius," Spencer said.

I couldn't resist giving a little bow.

Ben appeared behind me, and all three of us walked to the bus together. One of the combination lock girls arrived at the bus stop a few minutes later. I saw her look at me, then whisper something to her girlfriend.

As soon as I got home, Carly started pelting me with stories. Her class was going to study Alaska. And Hawaii. And go on a class trip to the natural history museum. And have a Hawaiian luau. And put on a play, *Hansel and Gretel.*

"How was *your* day, honey?" Mom asked, when Carly paused to catch her breath.

"Okay."

"Just okay?"

"No, it was good."

I wanted to tell her about the combination locks, but maybe that would sound stupid. I wasn't in second grade.

"I baked some cookies," she said. "It isn't the first day of school without home-baked cookies."

"Gingersnaps?" Carly asked.

Mom smiled and went to get a plate full of them. Gingersnaps were the best cookies she baked. I gobbled down two of them, still warm from the oven, soft and spicy, covered with crinkly sugar.

"We're going to keep journals!" Carly said. "We can write whatever we want in them. I've already written three pages in mine."

"That's wonderful, sweetie," Mom said.

I ate two more cookies and washed them down with a glass of cold milk. Between the combination locks and the gingersnaps, I felt hopeful about the new school year, about my mom, about everything.

But then, half an hour later, I walked by her bedroom and the door was closed. I knew she was sleeping. Ben's mother wasn't sleeping, Spencer's mother wasn't sleeping, nobody else's mother was asleep at four in the afternoon on a sunny August day. Something was wrong with my mother, and even a combination lock genius couldn't make it right.

4

"Today," said Mr. Pasta one morning early in September, "we will learn how to make the single most versatile and enticing of all breakfast foods."

"Pop-Tarts?" Spencer asked.

"No!" Mr. Pasta waved his spatula threateningly in Spencer's direction, but it was obvious he wasn't really angry. "Pop-Tarts are not food. They are two pieces of cardboard fastened together with overly sweet, artificially colored, fake fruity glue."

"I don't think he likes Pop-Tarts," Spencer whispered to Ben and me. One of the many good things about Food Fun was that Mr. Pasta let friends sit together and be on the same cooking team. It was a small class—eighteen students—and each team of three sat in one of the six cooking units, complete with our own table, stove, and sink.

"Would anyone care to make an *educated* guess?" Mr. Pasta asked.

Ben raised his hand. I knew Ben couldn't help

himself. It was just about impossible for Ben to know the correct answer and not volunteer it.

"Omelets?" Ben asked.

"Of course! Omelets with artichoke hearts, goat cheese, sun-dried tomatoes, smoked salmon, wild mushrooms . . ."

Mr. Pasta had a dreamy expression on his face, as if he could already taste each delicacy he was naming. All of them sounded terrible to me, especially the goat cheese. Not that I had ever eaten any, but there had to be a reason why most cheese came from cows.

"What about *normal* fillings?" Spencer asked.

"Such as?"

"Ham and cheese?"

"We will begin with ham and cheese," Mr. Pasta said regretfully. "Plain cheese for those of you who are vegetarians. I'm afraid the Western Hills school budget does not permit me to purchase artichokes and goat cheese. But I encourage all of you to try more exotic fillings at home."

Mr. Pasta began to demonstrate his omelet-making technique at the stove in the front of the class. "Now, the secret to a delectable omelet is to have just the right balance between eggs and filling."

I loved watching Mr. Pasta cook. He made everything look so easy, but so far, when Spencer, Ben, and I tried imitating him afterward, nothing turned out the way it should, even with Ben directing. And today we'd each be making our own omelet, as one omelet wasn't enough to feed three people.

Mr. Pasta flipped his omelet over in the pan with one deft flick of his wrist. I knew my own omelet would stick to the pan, or fall apart into scrambled eggs. I tried to pay attention to Mr. Pasta's quick, practiced motions. It would be great if I could surprise Mom and Carly with omelets for supper.

As it happened, when each team member took his turn, my omelet did disintegrate into scrambled eggs, as did Spencer's. But Ben's omelet was almost as impressive as if it had been produced by Mr. Pasta himself.

"Great job, Ben," Mr. Pasta said as he stopped by our station to inspect our progress.

We carried our plates to the table and began shoveling in big, eggy mouthfuls to beat the closing bell of class. Third period was definitely the best thing about sixth grade at Western Hills Middle School.

After school Ben had practice for the Western Hills cross-country team. I got off the bus with Spencer at the stop for his house, just one stop before mine, preparing myself mentally for the amount of cheerful chaos that I would find there.

For starters, Spencer's house was extremely messy. In the front hallway alone, I had to make my way around a gym bag, two bicycle tires, a half-full glass of Coke that someone had set on the floor, and a heap of every kind of shoe imaginable, no two matching shoes visible anywhere.

Then there was the noise level. At Spencer's house at least one TV would be blaring, usually two or three, all tuned to different channels, and a dog would be barking somewhere (Spencer's family had three). Louder than all the rest put together, Spencer's mom would be shouting at Spencer or his three older brothers.

I found it all oddly restful and reassuring.

Spencer's mother came to greet us. She was hardly any taller than Spencer, and weighed twice or three times as much.

"Did you leave this Coke glass by the front door?" she yelled at Spencer.

"No!" he yelled back.

"Who in his right mind would leave a Coke glass by the door where anybody could knock it over?" she shouted.

I couldn't help thinking: who in his right mind would leave two bicycle tires by the front door, and a couple hundred shoes?

Spencer's mother looked furious, but even as she kept on shouting that whoever had left the glass there had better be ready to get out the mop and clean up a big, sticky mess, she gave Spencer a hug and for good measure gave one to me, too.

"Well, don't just stand there! Come to the kitchen and get something to eat!" she ordered us.

I picked up the offending Coke glass and carried it into the kitchen, emptied it, and put it in the dishwasher. I knew everyone in Spencer's family would rather blame everyone else for leaving it there than pick it up and put it away.

"What do you want to eat?" Spencer asked. He threw open the pantry cupboard door, and we surveyed the jumbled contents of the bulging-full shelves. Every form of junk food known to man was available there.

"I'm sort of in the mood for Pop-Tarts," Spencer said. "How about you? Some nice tasty cardboard spread with fake fruity glue?"

"Sounds good to me," I agreed.

We each took two Pop-Tarts—no need for a plate at Spencer's house—and headed up to his room. I sprawled out on Spencer's unmade bed, and Spencer settled himself in a heap of pillows on the floor. A TV somewhere in the house blared out the cheers of the crowd at a baseball game; another TV was tuned to a war movie, with plenty of gunfire. I could hear Spencer's mother shouting, "Andrew, did you leave a Coke glass by the front door?"

"What Coke glass?" Andrew shouted back. "What are you talking about?"

I took the first bite of a chocolate fudge Pop-Tart. Mr. Pasta was right about a lot of things, but he was wrong about Pop-Tarts. Pop-Tarts were delicious.

My mom was sleeping when I came in the front door. Carly was next door at Jodie's house.

Welcome home, I thought.

I finished my L.A. homework quickly, making sure to put my name and class period in the upper left corner of the page. Miss Bellamy had given us time to finish our math homework in class. I didn't have anything for science or social studies. Practicing trombone was out of the question; I couldn't imagine breaking the silence with a B-flat major or F major scale.

At least Mom made a real dinner that night: spaghetti with sauce from a jar. I knew Mr. Pasta wouldn't have liked it. He didn't approve of pasta with store-bought sauce.

"So how was school?" she asked.

"We made omelets in Food Fun," I offered.

"How did they turn out?"

"Like scrambled eggs."

Mom laughed. "What about you, Carly Bug?"

"Jodie and I are making a book together," Carly said. "I'm writing the story, and she's drawing the pictures."

"What's it about?" Mom asked.

"It's called *The Magic Eraser*."

"What's magic about an eraser?" I asked.

"It can erase anything. Anything you don't want for there to be in the world, the eraser can erase it."

"Sounds good," Mom said, but I didn't think she was really listening.

"But what's the *plot*?" I pressed on. "The eraser erases all the bad things in the world, like war and poverty and cancer—the end? I mean, what happens after it all gets erased? Does the book just end with a bunch of empty pages?"

"We haven't finished it yet." Carly sounded defensive. "We *think* it's going to end with a picture of a flower. Just one little flower, with yellow petals."

"Everything in the world gets erased, and all that's left is one flower?"

"What's wrong, Cooper?" my mom asked, reaching over to pat Carly's hand. "What do you have against flowers?"

"Nothing."

Carly could never stay discouraged for more than half a minute. "Maybe Jodie and I will write a sequel: *The Magic Pencil*. The magic pencil can come along and write in all the new, good things. Do you think that's better, Cooper?"

"Sure," I said, ashamed of how I had responded before. "Keep working on it."

After Carly and I cleared the table and loaded the dishwasher, I hunted through my backpack for the notice I was supposed to bring home about the back-to-school night for parents on Wednesday, not that I thought my mother would have the energy to go this year. At least I could give her the notice and mark the date on the big calendar she had hanging on the kitchen wall, where all three of us were supposed to write down our activities.

I found a pen, but as I wrote "Cooper back-to-school night 6:30" on the calendar on Wednesday's square, I saw that Mom had already written "Dr. Leibowitz 1:30." I didn't know if I felt more relieved that she was seeing a doctor or worried about what kind of a doctor she was seeing.

I tried looking up Leibowitz in the phone book, and there was a listing for Leibowitz, Nancy, M.D., but that was all it said: it didn't give any other information.

On the computer upstairs in my bedroom, I typed in "Leibowitz Nancy MD," and then it came right up:

Nancy J. Leibowitz, M.D., Psychiatry

And then I knew.
My mother didn't have cancer.
My mother was crazy.

5

Gran-Dan always called Saturday morning at eight. There was something about the way he called on the same day at the same time that made it seem like a chore he was crossing off his list: 8:00, call Emily and the kids—done! He and I never had much to say to each other. He'd ask me about the weather and about school, and I'd say whether it was sunny or windy or snowy, and then I'd say that school was okay, and he would ask to talk to Carly or Mom.

That Saturday, I heard the phone ring while I was still in bed. I rolled over and pulled the covers over my head. Carly or Mom could talk to him first. But suddenly I wasn't sleepy anymore.

What if . . . what if I told Gran-Dan what I'd found out about Mom? That she was seeing a psychiatrist? I mean, if my mom was crazy, shouldn't some grownup family member know? Gran-Dan was the only other family member we had.

I got out of bed and scuffed my feet into my slippers.

After a week of still-summery September days, it had turned cold and the first frost was predicted. I found Carly on the couch in the living room, yakking away on the phone. She hardly paused for breath as she told Gran-Dan everything that had happened that week.

"We have an assembly every Monday, and at the assemblies different people in different classes get awards, you know, if they've done something special the week before, and I got an award for 'excellence in writing stories,' and Mrs. Brattle is going to let me publish one of my stories at the school publishing center, so I'll have a real book with my name on the cover, and a dedication page. I'm going to dedicate it to Jodie's cat, Skittles, because it's a story about a cat, a pirate cat, and Skittles gave me the idea for it, because she has kind of a black pirate patch around one eye, and at the end of the book there will be a page called 'About the Author' and it will say, 'Carly Harris lives in Colorado. She is seven years old. She has written many books, but this is the first one that got published.'"

There was a pause as Gran-Dan must have asked a question.

"No, she couldn't come to the assembly. But she likes the award and said she's going to get a frame for it and I can hang it up in my bedroom."

I waited as Carly proceeded to tell him the entire plot of *Priscilla the Pirate Cat*.

There was another pause on Carly's end of the phone. Then she said, "Sure. He's right here," and she handed the phone to me.

"Hey there, Coop," said Gran-Dan.

"Hi," I said. I walked into my room and shut the door behind me as I tried to think of what to say next. I climbed back into my bed, not realizing until now that I was shivering.

"So how's everything?" Gran-Dan asked.

"It's okay."

"I heard it's turning cold out there," Gran-Dan continued.

"Yeah. It's pretty cold this morning."

"What's new at school? What's your favorite subject so far?"

"Not much. Food Fun, I guess. The teacher, Mr. Pasta, I mean Mr. Costa, is pretty funny."

There was a pause. We had already gone through our two standard topics.

"One of my friends," I blurted out, then stopped.

"One of your friends what?"

"One of my friends broke his foot, playing soccer."

That was actually true, but it wasn't what I had meant to say.

"It'll heal," Gran-Dan said.

"There's another kid on my team? He's worried because his dad is seeing a psychiatrist." I purposely didn't say "his mom," so Gran-Dan wouldn't think I was talking about me. I wanted to see how he reacted before I said anything else.

"Everybody sees a psychiatrist nowadays," Gran-Dan said. "I guess people have to have something to throw their money away on. And somebody to boohoo to about their problems."

My mother knocked and then came into my room. I was glad I hadn't told Gran-Dan anything about her.

"Here's my mom," I said quickly. I handed her the phone and buried myself under the covers; I still had an hour before I had to get dressed to carpool to my soccer game with Ben.

At the game, Ben's whole family—his mom, his dad, his older sister—was there cheering from the sidelines. My mom and Carly weren't there, although they used to come all the time last year. Occasionally Ben's dad would shout some encouragement to me. "Good job, Coop!" I heard, when I made an especially good pass.

We won 3–2. Ben scored two of our three goals, of course. I didn't mind that Ben was the star of the team. He was so much better than the rest of us that there was no point in being jealous. Even though Ben did his best not to hog the ball, we wanted to pass to him all the time, because that was the way to win.

But I was jealous that Ben had a father. And a mother who wasn't crazy.

After lunch Mom disappeared into her bedroom with the door closed. I was going to do some homework—Miss Bellamy had assigned her favorite kind of word problems—but Carly dragged me into her room.

"I never gave you your deeds," she said.

"My deeds?" At first I thought she was talking about

Monopoly, but then she said, "To the Yukon. Remember? We each have four square inches. I brought yours home from Gran-Dan's. Here."

I took the four yellowed sheets of paper Carly handed to me. I had forgotten all about them.

"What are you going to do with yours?" she asked.

Do with them? "Save them, I guess."

"I was thinking we could put them together, your four inches and my four inches, and we could make a little country. We could call it Inchland. The people who live there are the Inchies. They're very tiny, so tiny that to them a square inch is as big as . . . Colorado?"

"That's too big. Maybe a square mile. For them, a square inch is like a square mile."

"Do you want to help me make a map? We can pick where the castle is, and the town—maybe one big town? It can be the capital of Inchland."

"Inchopolis," I suggested. I was getting interested in Carly's make-believe in spite of myself.

"I want it to have little, crooked streets," Carly said. "There are no cars in Inchland. In Inchland, it's still long ago. They haven't invented cars yet, or television, or electricity. The streets are lit with candles, so when the Inchies go for walks, everything is twinkling. Or maybe they use fireflies for the lights."

"The fireflies would be bigger than they are."

"Cooper! If the Inchies are tiny people, then their fireflies are tiny fireflies. Everything is tiny in Inchland."

Carly sat down at the table by her window. I sat

in the small chair facing her, feeling like a gigantic second grader. I was probably acting like a gigantic second grader, too.

"Do you want to make the map? Or do you want to draw the castle?" Carly asked.

"I'll do the map." I've always loved maps. I reached for Carly's wooden ruler.

"Remember, the streets are all crooked," Carly told me. "You're never sure exactly where you're going in Inchland. Even the Inchies get lost all the time. Only they don't call it getting lost. They call it getting surprised. And if they get too surprised, they can always look up and see the castle."

For the next hour, Carly and I sat at her table, drawing.

A week later, Spencer and I were at Ben's house on Sunday afternoon working together on a group project for social studies. We had to build an ancient Mayan pyramid. Spencer lay on the floor in Ben's family room, watching Ben and me cover the sturdy cardboard structure with a layer of clay. The next step, according to Ben's master plan, was to carve the clay into a steep staircase leading up to the cardboard temple perched on the pyramid's flat top.

"You could help, you know," Ben said to Spencer. He smoothed another thin slab of clay onto one side of the pyramid.

"Would you rather have me help and get a B, or do it all by yourselves and get an A?" Spencer asked.

"You can't mess this part up," Ben said. "I mean, we'll

do the steps, but you could at least do some of the clay. It's taking longer than I thought to get this covered."

"You're the one who wanted to make a *big* pyramid," Spencer reminded him. "It's not taking you as long as it took the Mayans."

"The Mayans didn't have two guys doing all the work while the other guy did nothing but still got the same grade," Ben pointed out.

While I listened to them squabble, I picked up a stick of brown clay and kneaded it for a minute or two until it was soft enough to mold. Then I flattened it to a quarter-inch thickness.

"Every single Mayan didn't work on the pyramids," Spencer protested. "Lots of Mayans did other things. Like . . . well, other things."

"Other things like lying on the floor?"

"Like designing a calendar," Spencer said. "That's right. I'm the guy who invents the calendar. My calendar has twelve months, one for each cycle of the moon. I'm calling this month El Septembero."

"The Mayans didn't speak Spanish, you dummy," Ben said. "America isn't going to be discovered for another thousand-plus years."

I grinned as I smoothed my clay onto the cardboard. Despite Spencer's laziness, it was worth having him in our group because he was so entertaining. Maybe the ancient Mayans had jesters to amuse the pyramid builders, too.

"What did the Mayans eat?" Spencer asked. "I might feel more like building a pyramid if I had some Mayan food to inspire me. Didn't Mr. Stuart say they ate pepperoni pizza?"

"Corn," Ben told him. "They ate corn."

"They had to have had something to go with it," Spencer said.

"Beans," I chimed in.

Spencer groaned.

I was softening my next stick of clay when Ben's mother came into the room. For a mother, she was amazingly pretty, slim and youthful, with chin-length blond hair.

"Are you boys getting hungry?" she asked.

"Yes!" Spencer shouted, rolling up to a sitting position as if to demonstrate his enthusiasm. "Building Mayan pyramids sure works up an appetite."

Ben glared at him.

"I mean, watching other people build pyramids sure works up an appetite."

Ben's mother laughed. "I hope you both can stay for dinner. Do you need to call your parents?"

"I already told my parents I was eating here," Spencer said.

She laughed again. "Cooper?"

"I'll call, but I'm sure it's okay."

Why wouldn't it be okay? Carly would be at Jodie's house, and my mom would be sleeping. Though I thought maybe she seemed a little better. I hadn't been snooping, exactly, but I had seen a bottle of pills on the nightstand next to her bed, and I had seen "Dr. Leibowitz 1:30" again on the calendar for next week.

No one answered the phone when I called, so I left a message, and that was that.

Dinner at Ben's house was the opposite of dinner at Spencer's house. Ben's family ate in the dining room, not the kitchen, with a tablecloth on the table. The food was delicious: grilled chicken breasts with mango salsa, fancy rice, and a dark green vegetable I didn't recognize, though it looked something like spinach.

"It's Swiss chard," Ben's mother said, apparently reading the question in my eyes.

Ben's father—as slim and good-looking as Ben's mother—said grace, and then everybody began to pass the serving plates along the table. Everyday dinners at Ben's house felt like Thanksgiving.

I used to think that Spencer's family and Ben's family were the two extremes, and my family was in the middle: not as loud, messy, and chaotic as Spencer's family; not as quiet, neat, and perfect as Ben's family. My family was the in-between family, the "just right" family, the normal family—well, as normal as a family could be that didn't have a dad.

That's what I used to think.

Ben's mother asked everyone a question in turn. Ben's father reported on his run; he was training for a marathon. Ben's older sister, Emma, shared a story from rehearsal; she was a singing and dancing fork in the high school production of *Beauty and the Beast*.

"Spencer, what's new at your house these days? Did Nate get his driver's license?"

"Yeah. But the day after he got it, he backed out of the garage too fast, and one of the side mirrors got knocked off, and now my dad won't let him drive anymore until he pays for a new one. Nate told him he never looks in the side mirrors anyway, and my dad got even madder, and said that that explained a lot."

Everyone laughed.

"Cooper, what about you? Tell your mom I haven't seen her out walking for the longest time. Is she busy getting ready for an art show, or is she just swamped with clients?"

"No." I tried to think of something to add, to make my answer funny and interesting like Spencer's.

Before the silence could become uncomfortable, Ben's mother said smoothly, "Well, tell her I said hi, will you?"

"Okay," I said.

Dessert was baked apples with real whipped cream, not whipped cream from a can or Cool Whip.

"I want to come live at Ben's house," Spencer said.

I knew Spencer said it as a compliment for the dinner. He couldn't really mean it. If Spencer lived at Ben's house, he'd have to clean his room, and give up junk food, and do his share on any future Mayan pyramids. If I lived at Ben's house, the meals would be better, but I'd miss seeing the walls covered with my mom's artwork, and hearing Carly's chatter.

I didn't want to live at Ben's house. I wanted to live at my own house, the way it used to be.

6

It rained the last weekend in September. It so seldom rained in Colorado that I loved a rainy day. Soccer was canceled, and on Saturday morning, I lay in bed listening to the steady rhythm of the rainfall on the roof, watching the rivulets of drops streaming down the window.

"Who wants French toast for breakfast?" I asked Mom and Carly, as I came into the kitchen after talking on the phone to Gran-Dan.

"Uh-oh," my mom said good-naturedly. "Are you volunteering to serve as chef?"

Her teasing tone made me grin. She was dressed, too, in a denim jumper with a flowery turtleneck underneath.

"Mom, my team got an A on our French toast," I informed her. It wasn't strictly true; Mr. Pasta didn't grade us on the quality of our cooking itself. But it was true that our team's French toast had been delicious. The question was whether it would be delicious without Ben to supervise.

"Can I help?" Carly asked. "What do we need to make it?"

"Bread and milk and eggs . . ." I tried to remember the rest. "And vanilla and sugar and cinnamon. Syrup to pour on it when it's done. Oh, and confectioners' sugar to sprinkle on top, if we have any."

While Carly hunted on the pantry shelves for the ingredients, I retrieved my morning binder from my backpack and found the handout with the recipe. There was a moment of panic, when Carly couldn't find any vanilla, but then it turned out to be hidden behind a large container of salt.

At the very last minute, as I was about to transfer the French toast to the plates, I remembered to slice up an orange from the fruit bowl to create a garnish. Mr. Pasta said that presentation was as important as taste. Food should please the eye as well as the mouth and the stomach.

"Oh, my!" Mom marveled when I brought the first plate to her at the kitchen table. "Cooper, this is beautiful!"

I savored every syrupy bite. Carly and Mom gobbled theirs all up, too.

"If I'm the family chef now, does this mean that I don't have to vacuum the living room?" I asked.

"The short answer is no. But I'll put on some reggae music, and while you're vacuuming I'll dust." She began humming a peppy tune as she grabbed a dustcloth from the kitchen drawer.

I stared at her. I hadn't seen her so energetic in months, not since the start of the summer.

Carly carried her dish over to the sink and, equally energetic, danced upstairs to change the sheets on her bed. Then, or so she had told us, she was going to work on her newest story, about a beautiful Hawaiian princess named Lu-ah-la-ah-li-ah.

I lingered at the table, not ready yet for the roar of the vacuum to disturb the coziness of the gray, gloomy morning.

"Carly told me that the princess in her story is all made out of fruit," I said. "She has a coconut for her head, and bananas for her arms, and a pineapple for her body."

Dustcloth in hand, Mom laughed and dropped back into her seat at the table again. "She sounds yummy."

I laughed, too. Then I said, "You seem different."

She hesitated. "I feel different. Oh, Coop, it's been a bad couple of months. It took so long for me to realize what was wrong, that I was depressed. I kept thinking, I have nothing to be depressed *about*. I have wonderful children and work that I love. But depression is a physical illness. If the chemical balance is wrong in your brain, you can't be happy, however good everything else is in your life."

"Are you taking medicine for it?" I asked, thinking of the bottle of pills beside her bed.

"Yes. It took a while for it to work, and I was getting more and more discouraged, but then last week I noticed that I felt . . . just more like my old self. Not so tired, not so hopeless. Cooper, honey, things are going to be different now. I can tell. It's all going to be better. I promise."

She reached out and gave me a long, enfolding hug. I fought tears as I hugged her back.

After a rousing, reggae-accompanied turn around the living room with the vacuum, I let Carly talk me into joining her at her small table to work on the maps and drawings for Inchland.

"This is the school the Inchie children go to," she told me. "It's a one-room schoolhouse like in *Little House on the Prairie*."

I studied Carly's picture. She had drawn the front of the school with a door, two windows, a chimney, and a bell.

"What kinds of things do they learn in school?" I asked, to play along.

"Well, reading and spelling, like we do here. But instead of geography they have inchography, where they study all about Inchland, how tall its mountains are, what its weather is like."

"What *is* its weather like?"

Carly thought for a minute. "They have four seasons, like we do, and it snows in winter, but not too much, because even an inch of snow would bury everything. It rains sometimes, but a drop of rain is enough for them to take their baths and water their plants."

"Do they have math in school?"

"Yes. It's mainly like our math, except that when they measure things, they don't have feet or yards or miles. They don't have anything bigger than an inch."

Carly selected a red crayon and began coloring in the shape of the schoolhouse. She poked the tip of her tongue out the way she did whenever she concentrated hard on doing something.

"In social studies, I bet they learn the history of Inchland," I suggested. "When it was discovered, how the Inchies came to live there."

Carly looked up from her coloring and shook her head emphatically. "Cooper, Inchland has never been discovered. The Inchies have always lived there. That's the most important thing for the Inchies, to keep it from being discovered. The Inchies are so little, and their country is so small. If big people found it, they could do something terrible—they could step on it, or treat the Inchies like toys and give them to careless big children to play with. Cooper, you have to promise you'll never tell anyone about Inchland."

"Sure," I agreed. Planning out a made-up country with a seven-year-old wasn't something I was going to talk about with my friends, that was for sure. "Does Jodie know about it?"

"No. Nobody knows but you and me. Don't tell anybody. Not Ben, not Spencer, nobody."

"Okay," I promised.

★　★　★

When I came home from school on Monday, all over the living room, the family room, the dining room, and spread out on the kitchen table were heaps of scarlet fabric, ropes of gold braid, and boxes of shiny gold buttons. Carly's ballet school was working on a program called "The March of the Toy Soldiers," and Mom had signed up to make toy soldier outfits for forty-five little ballerinas.

"Just the vests," she explained. "They can wear plain black pants with them. Two other moms are making the hats, out of cardboard spray-painted red, each with a large white feather on top—they're going to be darling. I'm the only mom who likes to sew, so I said I'd make the vests."

"Forty-five vests?"

"They'll go fast on the sewing machine, now that I have most of them cut out. Just a few seams, and then the trim—I guess that will take some time, and sewing on all the buttons. You and Carly can help."

"I don't know how to sew on buttons," I protested.

"Then it's high time you learned." She gave me a quick kiss. "We have plenty of time. The show isn't until a week from this coming Saturday. I have so many months of lost time to make up for. There aren't enough hours in the day to do all I want to do."

By the end of the week, I decided red and gold were the most hideous colors I had ever seen. I closed my eyes to go to sleep and saw patches of red and gold everywhere. Each vest had eight gold buttons. Eight times forty-five was three hundred sixty. Three hundred sixty buttons to sew! I tried to pretend I had homework to do, but Mom would find me in the basement rec room playing video games, and I'd be back at the dining room table with needle in hand.

"At least for the rest of your life you'll be able to sew on a button if you need to," she told me.

She enlisted Ben and Spencer in the effort as well. As the three of us were trying to sneak down the stairs to the basement one afternoon, she called out to us, "Boys!"

"Pretend you don't hear her," I whispered to them.

Fatally polite, Ben turned back.

"If each of you do three vests, that will be nine more done," she said with a smile.

The next thing I knew, all three of us were sewing on buttons, together with Carly, Jodie, and another of Carly's friends.

Ben sewed on two buttons in the time it took me to do one. Maybe it was a good idea to have Ben's help after all.

Spencer couldn't get the knack of threading a needle, so he used ridiculously long pieces of thread that got tangled on everything. He kept stabbing himself with the needle, and each puncture wound called for an elaborate performance to demonstrate the extent of his injury.

"Ow! Ouch! Mrs. Harris, I'm bleeding! I think I hit a vein! The blood is spurting!"

Then, a minute later, "Ow! I need a tetanus shot! I can tell I'm getting lockjaw!"

After half an hour, Spencer had sewed on exactly one button.

"Come see my button!" he crowed. "Mrs. Harris, tell me my button is the best!"

My mom came over to admire it. Her face fell. "Oh, Spencer—"

"What? I can take it."

"It's in the wrong place. See where the buttonhole is? The button has to line up with the buttonhole. You'll have to move it."

"Move it? How can I move it? It's sewed on!"

"You'll have to cut it off and sew it on again."

Spencer's anguished howls sent Carly and her second-grade friends into spasms of giggles.

"Instead of sewing on buttons, do you want to cut lengths of braid? Just measure out the braid, using this piece as a pattern, give one snip, and you're done. It's easy. Anybody can do it." Mom hesitated, giving a worried look at Spencer. "Well, maybe it isn't so easy."

"You mean, anybody can do it, except for Spencer," Spencer said.

The three little girls were giggling so much they could hardly keep sewing. My mom, Ben, and I were laughing, too. Ben laid another finished vest on the growing pile.

In Food Fun, our class was baking cookies to sell at a bake sale during the intermission of the Western Hills fall music extravaganza. The bake sale was a fund-raiser for all the Western Hills music programs: band, orchestra, and choir.

I had never realized there were so many different ways to make cookies. You could slice the dough from long rolled tubes; you could drop the dough onto the cookie tray by spoonfuls; you could shape the dough into little balls; you could roll the dough with a rolling pin and cut it into shapes with cookie cutters.

The only thing you couldn't do was eat the dough. That was Mr. Pasta's strictest rule.

"First, raw dough has raw eggs in it, and you can get salmonella poisoning from eating raw eggs. I don't want any phone calls from parents upset that their children have contracted salmonella poisoning in my cooking class. Second, raw dough is delicious, and if you start eating it, you won't be able to stop, and we won't have enough cookies to sell at the bake sale. Third, raw dough is very fattening." He patted his own round stomach.

That day we were making peanut butter cookies. For peanut butter cookies, we made dough balls and then flattened them with the tines of a fork, twice, to get a crisscross effect. I was our team's fork man. Ben made the balls, I flattened them, and Spencer placed them on the lightly greased cookie pan.

Criss! Cross! It was pleasant and satisfying work.

One flattened cookie disappeared en route to the pan.

"Spencer!" I hissed at him.

"I won't do it again. I couldn't resist just one. I know it was wrong. Ben, Cooper, I'm very, very, very sorry."

Spencer did look miserable. "If I die of salmonella poisoning, I deserve it. Don't even come to my funeral, okay?"

Ben whacked Spencer with the spatula.

The team at the next cooking station was all girls, including one of the girls I had helped on the first day of school with her combination lock, Lindsay.

"What did Spencer do?" Lindsay called over to us.

"Don't tell her," Spencer begged.

"Tell us!" Lindsay's best friend, Tamara, chimed in.

"No," Ben said. "He's been punished enough already by his own guilty conscience."

"Cooper will tell us, won't you, Cooper?" Lindsay asked.

I felt myself weakening. Once you had opened a combination lock for somebody, it gave the two of you a special bond, even though Lindsay and I had hardly spoken since. But I would never betray Spencer.

Mr. Pasta made his way over to our cooking station. "How are the peanut butter cookies coming along?" he asked. I knew he meant: is all this talking necessary?

"Fine," Ben said, gesturing to three filled pans ready to go into the preheated oven.

"Fine," Lindsay echoed. Before turning back to her cookies—I saw that she was the fork person on her team—she smiled over at us. I felt she was smiling mostly at me.

As we were sitting in social studies that afternoon doing some silent reading from our textbooks, Mr. Stuart walked from desk to desk in case anybody had questions.

All the sixth-grade Mayan pyramids were on display on top of the bookcases that stretched around the room. Our pyramid was definitely the biggest and the best. It was too bad that no one built real Mayan pyramids anymore: Ben could have had an amazing career ahead of him.

"You did a great job on your pyramid," Mr. Stuart told me.

"Ben thought up most of it," I confessed. Maybe it wasn't fair to Spencer to say it, but it was the truth.

"You need to give yourself more credit, Cooper," Mr. Stuart said. "I have a feeling you did your share."

I didn't think I deserved very much credit, but then again, I guessed I deserved more credit than Spencer did. It was nice of Mr. Stuart to say it, anyhow.

The Western Hills music extravaganza Friday night was a big success. The sixth-grade band sounded pretty good. We certainly played a lot better than my fifth-grade band last year, even if we didn't sound as good as the seventh and eighth graders. One trumpet came in too soon and earned a frown from the band teacher. Several of the clarinets squealed on their high notes. But all in all, it was a decent performance.

The sale of the Food Fun cookies raised over three

hundred dollars. My mom bought a plate of frosted butter cookies cut in the shapes of stars and bells, and a plate of peanut butter cookies. I studied the cookies critically; I didn't recognize the crisscross marks as mine, but admittedly it was impossible to tell. I sort of hoped they were Lindsay's.

Carly's ballet recital was on Saturday afternoon. I felt a surge of pride as the forty-five ballerina toy soldiers marched out onto the stage wearing their costumes. I wondered how many people in the audience knew the work that had gone into sewing on all those shiny gold buttons, the blood that had been shed. I was glad when, at the end of the performance, the costume-making moms were all handed big bouquets of flowers.

Right then I thought that everything was going to be okay with my mom. I really did.

7

Chicken soup," Mr. Pasta said, one Monday late in October. His tone was hushed and reverent, as if he were about to say a prayer. "Imagine a bitter winter day. You are home in bed with the sniffles and a sore throat and a fever of 101.2. Then, in comes your mother to your bedroom, bearing a tray. On the tray is a bowl of chicken soup."

He sighed deeply. Then he collected himself. "Today, my young friends, *you* will be making chicken soup."

Spencer raised his hand.

"Yes, Spencer?" Mr. Pasta asked with mock weariness.

"Why can't you just heat up some chicken soup out of a can?"

"Some questions," Mr. Pasta said, "I refuse even to answer."

Mr. Pasta continued talking about the importance of something called stock—the watery part of the soup,

I gathered. The secret to making perfect chicken soup lay in first making perfect chicken stock.

Ben handed me a bunch of celery to chop up and tossed Spencer a large onion. Spencer missed the catch, and the onion rolled across the floor into Lindsay's cooking station.

Lindsay picked it up, but instead of tossing it back, she came over and handed it to me. I didn't know if she thought I had been the one who missed the catch or if she just felt like handing the onion to me rather than to Spencer.

"I don't want to chop the onion," Spencer said. "I hate chopping onions. My eyes will water, and my nose will run, and it will drip onto everything, and instead of chicken stock, we'll have—"

"Fine," Ben interrupted, before Spencer could add any more unappetizing details. "I'll chop the onion. You can cut up the chicken."

"I don't want to cut up the chicken. I hate cutting up dead things." Spencer pointed to the raw chicken on the plate Ben had set on our counter. "Look, you can see the blood!"

I caught Lindsay's eye, and we both started giggling.

Now Ben was starting to look irritated. "Cooper, will *you* do the onion *or* the chicken, so Spencer can do the celery?"

"Sure." Still clutching the onion, with my free hand I shoved the celery toward Spencer. I didn't mind chopping the onion. I wished Lindsay could stay to watch me chop it, not that chopping an onion was as glamorous as opening a combination lock. But she just shook her head at Spencer's squeamishness and returned to her own station to chop an onion of her own.

After school on Friday, Spencer and I were supposed to be working on our report on Uruguay for social studies. For this project, we could only work alone or in pairs. Ben had volunteered to be the one working alone, so Spencer and I were actually going to have to do everything ourselves.

"Can we go to your house?" I asked as we were getting our coats from our lockers after the last bell. With my mom's new quilt project, our place looked like a fabric store—an extremely messy and cluttered fabric store. When she had made quilts before, her studio was always a disaster area, but not the whole house.

"At my house people are always yelling," Spencer said.

"Well, at my house people are always . . . quilting," I countered. It wasn't what I meant, but I didn't know how else to say it.

Spencer laughed. "I pick quilting."

So we went to my house.

All over the living room lay heaps of fabric, in every shade of red and purple.

"Wow," Spencer said. "Your mother must be making a really *big* quilt."

"She says she has to study the fabric first, look at the colors to see which ones go together."

"Is it okay to step on the cloth?"

It would have been impossible not to. "Yeah. Just take off your shoes first."

"Boys!" my mom called to us from the top of the stairs. "Do you want a snack?"

As she started down the stairs toward us, I saw her arms, bare to the elbow. They were bright red. For a fleeting second I thought of blood.

"Mom—"

"I decided to dye my own fabric," she announced gaily. "Don't faint if you use the bathroom upstairs. I haven't murdered anybody."

I looked away.

In the kitchen, Spencer and I helped ourselves to sharp cheddar cheese and Ritz crackers, and tall glasses of apple cider. Then we walked across a carpet of thickly layered scarlet and violet fabric up the stairs to my room. I peeked into the bathroom: the water in the tub was crimson.

"Mom," I said as she was bending over the tub. "The house is a mess."

"Don't worry. Once the quilt is finished, the house will be back to normal in a jiffy."

"When does it have to be done by?"

"In two weeks."

"But you haven't even started it yet."

She stared at me. "What do you mean, I haven't started it yet? What do you think I'm doing right now? Why do you think there's fabric all over the house?

Honey, quilting is all about *color*. I can't do anything else on the quilt until I get the colors right."

I gave up. In my room, I found Spencer sprawled on my bed, his mouth full of cheese and crackers. I settled myself at my desk and took a long sip of cider.

"I see what you mean about quilting," Spencer said once he had devoured what was left on his plate.

"It's pretty bad."

"Yelling is pretty bad, too. And now we have to work on our report on Uruguay. Which do you think is worse: quilting, yelling, or Uruguay?"

"They're all bad," I said.

"Are you going to eat the rest of your snack?" Spencer asked.

"No. Help yourself."

I put my plate on the bed next to Spencer. Then I turned on my computer and sadly Googled Uruguay.

"I'm going to draw how Inchland looks when it's covered in snow," Carly told me the next evening as she and I sat together in her room while Mom was out doing some shopping. The first snow of the year was forecast for tonight. I decided that I'd try to finish the map of Inchopolis.

Carly drew for a few minutes in silence. Then she said, "Inchland has a king, King Inchard. The queen's name is Queen Incharina. I'm drawing the princess, Princess Inchitella. She is seven years old, just like I am. She is very lonely, because she has no brothers and

64

sisters, and no friends, either, because there are no other princesses who live nearby that she can be friends with."

"Can't she be friends with regular people?"

"She wants to, but her parents won't let her. They say that a princess has to have friends who are of royal blood. They're very strict."

"What does this have to do with snow?" I asked. "I thought you were drawing Inchland in the snow."

"All the other children are outside playing in the snow. Princess Inchitella wants to play with them, but she can't. So she's watching them from the window in the highest tower in the castle. She's so lonely she starts to cry, and when she cries, her tears freeze onto her cheeks like diamonds. You know, because she has the window open. Only when a princess's tears freeze, they don't just get hard like diamonds. They turn into diamonds. Two tears roll down each cheek, so that means she has four diamonds, all her own."

"Didn't she already have heaps of diamonds? If she's a princess?"

"Of course. But all those other diamonds really belong to her parents. Like if you and I had diamonds, they'd really belong to Mom, don't you think? These diamonds belong to her, just to Princess Inchitella, because she cried them out of her own eyes."

"Then what happens?" I asked, interested in Carly's story in spite of myself.

"Then," Carly said solemnly, "she takes her four diamonds and wraps them up in her royal silk handkerchief, and she puts on her warmest coat and hat and warmest boots and mittens. And she runs away."

"Doesn't anybody stop her?"

"No. All the royal servants are outside shoveling snow. Nobody sees her go."

"Not even King Inchard and Queen Incharina?"

"Nobody," Carly said. "Nobody at all."

8

I was on the phone in the living room the next Saturday, telling Gran-Dan that it might snow again and that school was fine. To stall for a minute before he'd ask to talk to Mom, I told him about the upcoming project in Food Fun, making dinner for the homeless people at the Community Table.

"Must be nice," Gran-Dan said. "Don't have a job, don't work, don't earn any money, and then get a bunch of kind souls to come cook dinner for you every night."

"Maybe they can't find jobs," I said.

"Maybe they drink too much to look for one."

I gave up. "Anyway, that's what we're doing in Food Fun."

"Well, it's always a good thing to learn how to cook. I still miss your Gran-Ellen's meals something terrible."

I knew he missed a lot more than her meals, but that kind of thing was hard for Gran-Dan to say.

I had been dreading what Gran-Dan said next: "Now, put me on the phone to your mother."

"She's out. Doing errands." I didn't want to admit that she was out shopping: her favorite fabric store was having a huge sale, with the doors opening an hour early. If she bought any more fabric, I was going to hole myself up in my room and never come out. There would be no place else for me to be.

"At eight o'clock in the morning? Isn't everything closed? What kinds of errands can she be doing at this time of day?"

"I don't know." I felt a flash of sympathy for Mom. Last summer Gran-Dan had been upset with her because she slept so late; now he was on her case because she was up and about so early.

"I guess I should go," I said.

"Okay, Cooper. Have fun cooking. Tell your mom I called. And tell those bums to get a job!"

I knew he meant it to be a funny line, but I didn't think it was funny.

An hour later Mom returned home, coming in from the garage burdened with three enormous shopping bags.

I was about to escape to my room when she called out to me. "Coop, honey, I need your help. I can't carry everything in all by myself."

"There's more?" I asked. She had always been so worried about money, turning the thermostat down to save on the heating bills, clipping coupons for the grocery store, driving an ancient car with a hundred fifty thousand miles on it.

She looked irritated. "Yes, there's more. There's a lot

more. I've never skimped on buying your school supplies. Well, these are my work supplies."

"Never mind. I didn't say anything." I headed out to the car and lugged in the four remaining bags, bulging with fabric.

"Where should I put them? In your studio?" Every surface there was covered with the work in progress on the competition quilt.

She waved her hand. "For now, just put them anywhere."

I dropped them on the floor next to the kitchen table, which was still buried under bolts of red and purple fabric, artwork of Carly's that Mom wanted to frame, two weeks' worth of newspapers, and stacks of unopened junk mail. Peeking out from underneath it all were scraps of felt and gold braid left over from the toy soldier costume project.

One of the fabric bags, stuffed too full, tipped over. As I righted it, I picked up the credit card receipt, which had fallen onto the floor. $637.21. My mother had spent six hundred dollars at one store in one morning.

I shouldn't have said what I said next. "Mom, are you sure you can afford this? I mean, you haven't been doing much paid work lately—"

She cut me off. "And how much paid work have you been doing lately? Cooper, when it comes to making art, the question isn't: can you afford to do it? The question is: can you afford not to?"

I gave up and fled to join Carly in Inchland.

Carly was sitting at her little table, drawings spread out in front of her.

"What's happening in Inchland?" I asked.

"Remember how the princess ran away? After the snowstorm? The snow is all melted here, but it's still snowing in Inchland, and the princess is cold and hungry and has no place to sleep."

"Why doesn't she go back to the castle?"

Carly didn't answer for a minute. She reached for a piece of paper and her colored pencil. "She can't. King Inchard and Queen Incharina will be so angry. And everything will be just the way it was before. She'll still be lonely, with no friends."

I remembered something. "Doesn't she have diamonds with her? Can't she spend them to buy some food?"

It was too bad Mom didn't have some diamonds to pay her credit card bill.

"She tries." Carly drew the outside of a building that looked like a shop. "She goes to the bakery to buy some bread, but when she takes out a diamond to pay for it, the man in the store laughs at her. I mean, Cooper, what if you went to King Soopers to buy some bread and tried to pay with a diamond?"

"The man probably thinks it's fake," I said.

"How *could* he think it was real? Nobody carries around real diamonds in their pockets."

"The same thing happens when she goes to the inn

to get a room," I continued. "They send her away, even though it's still snowing."

"But there's a boy who works at the inn, a poor, ragged boy who is seven years old, just like Inchitella. His name is . . ."

"Parsley." The name came to me suddenly.

"Parsley sneaks out to follow Inchitella, and he tells her she can sleep in the stable, like Mary and Joseph, when there was no room for them at the inn. Parsley helps her make a little, tiny bed of straw, covered with an old blanket."

"He gives her food, too, that the innkeeper was going to throw away. Some crusts of bread, and half an apple, and—"

"Barley soup. In an old, broken bowl. It tastes so good because it's hot and steamy, and Inchitella is so cold."

"Is she sad, having to sleep in the stable?" I asked.

"No. She's happy. All her life people have waited on her and given her everything, because she was a princess. Parsley doesn't know she's a princess. He gives her the blanket and the barley soup just to be kind. No one has ever been kind like that to her before. So that's where she lives now."

I started working on the floor plan of the little stable house, showing where all the furniture would go. Carly drew a picture of Inchitella and Parsley holding hands.

"Are they going to get married?" I asked.

"Cooper, they're only seven! But maybe someday."

I knew I should be working on my report on Uruguay, but it was better to stay in Inchland with Carly, where outside the princess's snug little stable house, the soft Inchland snow kept silently falling.

The second grade was putting on the play *Hansel and Gretel*. When I arrived home from school on Wednesday afternoon, Carly was full of news about it.

"We're having *auditions*—is that the word, Cooper? Like real actors for a real play. You have to stay after school and read lines for Mrs. Brattle. And then, after everybody has read, she's going to post a list that tells if you got the part or not. Don't you think that would be the scariest thing that could ever happen to you? Looking at the list to see if your name is on it? When everyone else is looking at it, too?"

"I don't think I approve of auditions in the second grade," Mom said, as she handed Carly a cup of hot chocolate and set a plate of gingersnaps on the one remaining empty corner of the kitchen table, shoving aside the dirty dishes left over from breakfast that morning. "You have the rest of your life to have stress like that. Why not just give everybody a part?"

I agreed. I couldn't bear the idea of Carly waiting for the cast list to be posted, and then maybe finding out that she didn't get any part at all.

"Everybody *is* going to get a part," Carly said, "but some of the parts are little, and some of the parts are big. The little parts are the birds who eat the bread crumbs, and squirrels, and two friendly foxes, and a bear. They help Hansel and Gretel in the woods. The big parts are Hansel, Gretel, the father, the stepmother, and the witch."

"What part do you want?" I asked.

"Gretel. Most of the girls want to be Gretel. Jodie wants to be the witch. I'm glad Jodie doesn't want to be Gretel, because it would be awful if you and your best friend wanted the same part and only one of you could get it, don't you think? But it will still be pretty awful if Jodie is the witch and I'm a bird. But I'll act happy for her."

"Maybe you'll be Gretel and Jodie will be a bird," I suggested.

"No, Jodie will definitely be the witch. You should hear her say, 'Nibble, nibble, little mousie. Who's that nibbling at my housie?' It would make your blood run *cold*."

I doubted that greatly.

"*You* haven't nibbled a bite," Mom told Carly. "Drink your hot chocolate before it gets cold. Cooper, what's new and exciting for you at school these days?"

"Nothing."

"What are you doing in Food Fun?"

"We're going to cook dinner at the Community Table next week. For homeless people. Or anybody who needs a free dinner. Each Food Fun class has a different night. My class has Tuesday. We're going to make spaghetti and salad and garlic bread. We're not making desserts, because we'll have cakes and pies donated by one of the big grocery stores."

"What a wonderful idea! I'm so glad you're doing something to help those poor, desperate people. Can parents help?"

I wanted to say no, but the fact was that in my backpack at that very moment was a permission slip I was supposed to give to her, and right on the permission slip was a box where parents could sign up to assist.

"Yeah, but—"

"But what?"

"I think Mr. Pasta's going to end up with too many parents who want to help. He only needs a few."

Mom laughed. "You mean you don't want to be embarrassed by having your mother there. Right? I was in middle school once myself, and I remember thinking I'd die if my parents helped out at school with anything."

"So you won't sign up to help?" I was relieved that she understood.

"No! Of course I'm going to sign up to help; Carly can spend the evening with Jodie. I meant that you won't be the first or last middle school kid to be embarrassed by your parent. I was embarrassed by my parents, and I'm sure someday your kids will be embarrassed by you."

I sighed and pulled the permission slip out of my backpack. It might be true that all kids were embarrassed by their parents. But it was also true that some parents were more embarrassing than others.

Still, at least my mom cared about homeless people, unlike Gran-Dan. All we were going to be doing was making spaghetti and putting it on plates. There was no reason to be nervous about Mom being there. No reason at all.

9

Dinner at the Community Table started out all right. As soon as the final bell rang, the kids from our Food Fun class went by school bus with Mr. Pasta to the church that hosted the dinner. The parent helpers were supposed to meet us there, but Mom was late.

Mr. Pasta handed out jobs from his long printed list. Spencer took cutting up desserts. Ben took chopping onions. "I need two people to chop the green peppers," Mr. Pasta said.

"I'll do it," I said.

"Me, too," Lindsay said.

I felt myself flushing. Had Lindsay volunteered for the green peppers because she wanted to chop green peppers, or because she wanted to chop green peppers with *me*?

Either way, there we stood, side by side, facing a huge bag of peppers. Wordlessly we ran them under cold water and then began slicing them in half, scooping out the seeds, and cutting them into small pieces.

I tried to think of something to say. "Your pieces are smaller than mine," I observed.

Lindsay studied my cutting board. "I think that's okay."

"They're all going to get mixed up together anyway," I agreed. "Your peppers and mine." I blushed again. I hoped she didn't think I was trying to be romantic.

"This pepper is funny-looking." Lindsay held up a pepper that had two dents that looked sort of like eyes, and a bulge beneath them that resembled a nose.

"We should give it a name," I suggested.

"Like what?"

"Peter Pepper?" It was a dumb, obvious name, but I had never been asked to come up with a name for a pepper before.

"Hi, Peter," Lindsay said to the pepper.

"Hi, Lindsay," I made the pepper say. I had never made a voice for a pepper before, either.

"Now I don't want to cut him up," Lindsay said.

"We don't have to. The sauce will taste the same without him."

"We could rescue him!"

"Take him home!"

"He could be our pet!"

"Our Peter Pepper pet!"

We were both laughing now.

From the stove, Mr. Pasta called out, "Onions! Peppers! Garlic!" Still giggling, Lindsay and I hastily chopped up the remaining peppers under Peter Pepper's watchful gaze. We kept him apart from all the other peppers, so we wouldn't chop him up by mistake. I had never dreamed I could have so much fondness for a vegetable.

By five o'clock the huge cauldron of sauce was bubbling on the stove, a vat of spaghetti had been boiled and drained, the garlic bread was staying warm in the oven, and the salad was tossed. For the first time I became aware that the dining room beyond the kitchen had filled up with perhaps a hundred people waiting to be served. The man in charge of the Community Table welcomed everyone, led a short moment of silence, and then the homeless people lined up for their food.

I was relieved not to be one of the kids doing the serving. It had been hard enough making conversation with Lindsay and Peter Pepper. I had never tried to talk to anybody who was homeless. But as the diners filed through the serving line, they didn't seem like homeless people, and they certainly didn't seem like lazy bums. They just seemed like people. Most were men, but some were women. They joked about the weather, commented on the food, thanked the servers for helping.

"Hi, honey." I whirled around. It was my mother. "I'm sorry I'm late. What should I be doing?"

Mr. Pasta overheard the question. "You and Cooper can take the dessert carts around."

Two carts held a selection of donated cakes and pies cut up into pieces. I took one cart, and Mom took the other. I wheeled my cart silently from table to table, but Mom talked to everybody. It was nice to talk to people, I reminded myself. She was just being friendly.

But I could hear her across the room, talking too loud, too fast. She was telling one homeless man about her quilts, the show she was going to enter, how much she loved color. I couldn't hear what the man replied.

"Exactly!" Her voice rose above the hubbub of the crowded hall. "I knew you were an artist, too!"

A woman with two missing front teeth took the last piece of pie from my cart. I had just begun wheeling the empty cart back to the kitchen when I heard someone clinking a spoon against a glass to get everybody's attention.

"Excuse me!" my mom called out. "I have an announcement to make! I'm going to be organizing a Community Table art show. Art by and about the homeless."

What?

"I know that some of you here are artists—I mean, everybody is an artist in some way, right? So I'm inviting you to create your own artwork and submit it for the show."

The man she had been talking to asked a question, but I couldn't hear what he said.

"Art in any medium—painting, sculpture, ceramics, fabric art, you name it. Preference will be given to pieces that illuminate the experience of homelessness."

The Community Table leader approached her and said something in a low voice. He probably was surprised to find that his organization was now sponsoring an art show.

"Call me at home," she continued, "and I'll give you

the details, once I have them." She recited her name and our home phone number.

Back in the kitchen, I was put to work drying dishes with Ben and Spencer. Lindsay had been helping to serve, but the long line of diners had finally come to an end, so she joined the crew of dryers.

"Your mom is brave," she said.

"Yeah," I said. That was one way of looking at it.

"Are you going to help her with the art show? I can help, too. I mean, if you need help."

"Well . . ."

"Well, what?"

I thought of the still unfinished quilt for the quilt show; the competition deadline had come and gone. "My mother's ideas don't always end up happening," I told her. These days they didn't.

"At least she has ideas," Lindsay said.

I didn't know how to reply to that. I dried the rest of the mugs from the dishwasher while Lindsay dried a stack of trays. Maybe we would all be lucky and the art show idea wouldn't happen, either.

But I couldn't shake the memory of my mom there with all the homeless strangers, acting like they were her best friends in the whole world, words and ideas pouring out of her in a flood, washing over everybody in the room. Washing over me.

On Wednesday, Carly was going to find out what part she was getting in the play. I walked home more quickly than usual from the bus stop, though if Carly was going to be in tears, I didn't particularly want to see it. Even when my mom had been depressed for so long, I had hardly ever prayed that she would get better. It somehow had seemed too big a prayer for even God to handle. But I prayed now: "Dear God, please don't let Carly be a bird."

As soon as I came in the front door, I knew it was all right. Carly ran up to me, her face radiant.

"I'm Gretel!" she announced unnecessarily. "And Jodie is the witch!"

"And I'm building the set!" my mom chimed in as she followed behind Carly.

I felt a twinge of uneasiness. "When is the play?"

"The first week in December!" Carly said. "We have four weeks of rehearsal. I already know most of my lines. I thought maybe it was bad luck to learn them ahead of time, but I learned them anyway. Do you want to hear them, Cooper? I have the very first line in the whole play. I hold my stomach and I say, 'Hansel, I'm hungry.' Because we're poor, you know, and our parents have no money to buy food to feed us."

"That's great," I said. "You can say the rest for me later." I wasn't worried about Carly learning her lines in time for the play. I was worried about my mother finishing the set in time for the play. "What kind of set is it going to be?"

"I'll need to make the witch's gingerbread house, and the cage where Hansel is fattened to be eaten, and the oven."

"That's a lot."

"Well, I don't see how you could stage *Hansel and Gretel* with less, do you? Don't worry, honey, it will go fast. I can get started on it as soon as I finish my quilt for the quilt show."

"I thought you missed the deadline for the quilt show."

"For the *other* quilt show. And I need to apply for a grant to get funding for 'Homeless, Not Voiceless'— that's what I'm calling the art show for the Community Table. Don't look so panicked, Cooper. Have you ever heard the saying 'If you want something done, ask a busy person'?"

I hadn't. It seemed like a dumb saying. She was in a good mood, so I took a chance. "What about the saying 'Don't bite off more than you can chew'?"

She laughed. "Funny you should say that. I learned a little poem once that went like this: 'Bite off more than you can chew, and chew it. Plan for more than you can do, and do it. Hitch your wagon to a star, keep your seat, and there you are!'"

Carly loved the poem and made Mom say it again.

I wanted to ask, *But what if you* don't *keep your seat? Then what?* But I had said enough already.

Carly and I had started building a little stable house for Princess Inchitella. The roof was made of toothpicks, glued together, with tufts of cotton covering it for snow. Carly had taken a pinch or two of lint from the dryer and used it to stuff a tiny mattress made of two felt rectangles stitched together, and an even tinier pillow. Inchitella's table was made of a penny propped up on legs sawed from a toothpick with my Swiss Army knife. Instead of chairs, Inchitella and Parsley had teeny stools made from brass fasteners. A seashell the size of my pinkie nail served as their sink.

I had wondered if Carly would trim the stable with Hansel-and-Gretel-style candy decorations, but the only way the play rehearsals affected Inchland was that Inchitella and Parsley had become friends with a flock of kindly birds.

"The birds bring them food," Carly explained Thursday after school, as I was trying to construct a miniature stone fireplace out of a cupful of gravel collected from the driveway.

"Worms?"

"Of course not, silly. Nuts and berries. Even birdseed is good. Inchitella grinds it into flour to make tiny loaves of brown bread. She makes jam from the berries. And the bees bring her some of their honey."

"In the winter?" I asked. "I thought bees made honey in the summer."

"They make it in the summer, and then they eat it in the winter."

I had no idea if Carly's statement was true, but it sounded plausible enough.

"Nothing has ever tasted so good to Inchitella as that homemade brown bread spread with honey," Carly continued. "At the castle she used to eat . . . What are some fancy foods, Cooper?"

I tried to remember Mr. Pasta's favorite delicacies. "Artichoke hearts. Smoked salmon."

"At the castle she used to eat artichoke hearts and smoked salmon, all by herself, on silver plates edged with gold, and she'd wipe her mouth on a silken napkin. But she's happier eating brown bread and honey with Parsley."

"Who are you talking about?"

I looked up from sorting through the gravel to find Mom standing beside me, gazing down at my work.

"Inchitella," Carly said. "The princess of Inchland. Remember Gran-Dan's deeds?"

Mom looked blank.

"To one square inch of the Yukon? Well, Cooper and I put our square inches together, and we've made them into a country called Inchland. And it has a king named King Inchard, and a queen named Queen Incharina, and a princess named Princess Inchitella, and Princess Inchitella has run away, and now she lives in a stable, and Cooper and I are making the stable."

"You have a wonderful imagination, Carly," Mom said, when my sister paused for breath. "Both of you do. I'm so proud of your stories, Carly, and Cooper, of your talent for art. What are you making there, Coop?"

"Nothing," I said. I shielded my work on the gravel fireplace with my hand. "I'm just messing around."

"I have an idea," Mom said. "You could make plates

84

for Inchitella and Parsley using a hole punch on laminated paper, or colored plastic, the kind from a report cover for school."

It was a good idea, but I didn't want anybody else's good ideas. Carly and I had enough good ideas of our own.

"I'll go look for one," Mom volunteered. "I know we have heaps of plastic covers around here somewhere."

"Actually," I said, "we were just finishing up for today. I have to practice my trombone. And then I have homework. And Carly has homework, too, don't you, Carly?"

"Yes, but we can make the plates first, can't we, Cooper?"

"We'll make them tomorrow."

"And you could make drinking glasses by snipping off the ends of plastic straws," Mom continued.

"I have to go," I said. I didn't want to be mean, so I added, "Big test on commas tomorrow for Alpert."

I left for my room, but not before I heard her say, "What could they use for a bathtub? I know—a peanut shell!"

I played my trombone extra loud so I wouldn't hear Carly's high, piercing voice telling Mom more about Inchland, and Mom's voice, too loud, too fast, too enthusiastic in reply.

Wasn't Carly the one who had wanted to keep Inchland secret? Wasn't she the one who said that something terrible could happen if big people ever discovered it?

10

Of the three of us, Ben's birthday came first, in October, then Spencer's the middle of November, and finally me in May. Ben had had a big party on his twelfth birthday—a dozen guys going to see the football game at the university. Spencer's party was just a sleepover for the three of us.

I walked over to Spencer's around five o'clock with my sleeping bag, not that I planned to sleep, and my toothbrush, not that I planned to brush my teeth.

It now seemed unbelievable that I had ever considered Spencer's house messy. Compared to my own house these days, Spencer's was a model of neatness. You could sit on any couch without having to move heaps of fabric or quilting magazines. You could walk across vast expanses of bare floor—dodging the occasional pair of shoes or empty pizza box, to be sure. Dirty dishes filled the sink, but not the kitchen counters. Being at Spencer's felt almost like being at Ben's.

Ben arrived soon afterward, and we claimed the

game system in the basement rec room, using Spencer's birthday privileges to banish his older brothers. Around seven we joined Spencer's family for huge quantities of pizza. As usual, everyone was shouting rather than talking, grabbing rather than reaching, jostling each other to get the last piece of sausage and pepperoni. Spencer's dogs barked incessantly. It was all good-natured and jolly.

Spencer's cake was lit: twelve candles. In another year we would all be thirteen: teenagers. Spencer's mom started singing "Happy Birthday to You" in a high, fake-operatic voice. Spencer's dad drowned her out with his booming bass. One of Spencer's brothers added lyrics I had never heard before: not the standard "Happy birthday to you, you live in a zoo, you look like a monkey, and you smell like one, too," but something that had "You just stepped in poo" as one of the lines, and "You smell like dog doo" as another. All three dogs were howling, each in a different key.

Spencer blew out the candles in one breath, so he'd get his wish, whatever it was.

I wasn't sure what I would have wished if it had been my birthday and not Spencer's. I wished my mom would finally finish her quilt project and not start another one; I wished we would get an A on our report about Uruguay.

Over the din, the phone rang. Four boys dove at once to answer it.

"I think it's for you." Spencer's brother Nate tossed the phone to me. Surprised that anyone would be calling me at Spencer's, I managed to catch the phone before it landed in Spencer's birthday cake. I wondered how Spencer could be so bad at catching, given all the items that were tossed at him by his brothers.

"Hello?" I said.

I could barely hear the soft voice at the other end.

"Hello?" I said again.

"Hi, Cooper, it's me. Carly."

"What's wrong?"

I strained to hear her answer.

"Mom's not here, and I went over to Jodie's house, and nobody's there, either, and I'm all alone, and I'm scared, Cooper."

"What do you mean, Mom's not there?" Mom never left Carly alone; Carly was only seven, she was too young to be left at home by herself.

"She's not here," Carly said again. "I was up in my room coloring, and when I came downstairs she was gone. I couldn't find her anywhere in the house, and then I looked in the garage, and the car is gone, and Spencer's phone number was on the list on the bulletin board, so I tried to call you, and this lady said I had the wrong number, and I tried again, and, Cooper, can you come home?"

"I'll be right there," I said, and hung up.

What could have happened to make Mom leave like that? Maybe she had cut her hand with her sharp sewing scissors and had to drive to the emergency room, bleeding so bad she forgot all about Carly, or maybe she didn't want to scare Carly with the sight of the blood. I had gone to the emergency room once, when I broke my arm back in third grade, and it took forever once you got there.

"I have to go home," I told Spencer.

"Is something wrong?" Spencer's mother asked.

"No," I lied. "I just have to go home. My mother told Carly to call me and tell me to come. She needs me to help with something."

"You haven't even eaten your cake!"

"That's okay. I'm pretty full from the pizza."

All I wanted was to go, but I waited while Spencer's mom sliced three pieces of birthday cake and wrapped them up for me in aluminum foil.

"Can you come back later? After you finish help-ing?" Spencer said. "We're going to watch *Night of the Living Dead* and then another movie I got about mummies."

"I'll try," I promised, but I took my sleeping bag with me, just in case. After jogging the first block, with my sleeping bag bumping against my leg, I realized that I had forgotten the foil-wrapped plate of cake, but that didn't matter. What mattered was getting home to Carly.

As I entered the front door, I saw her, huddled on the couch. She ran into my arms.

"Oh, Cooper!"

"It's okay. See? I'm here now, and everything's fine."

I heard Mom's car pulling into the garage. I expected

to see her race into the room, pale with worry, her hand swaddled in a huge bandage, or even in a cast, but in she strolled, looking just like her regular self.

"What?" she said when she caught sight of my angry face.

"Where were you?"

"I just ran out to do an errand."

"Carly was here all by herself!"

Mom looked irritated. "She can be alone for ten minutes, Cooper. She's alone longer than that when she walks by herself to and from school."

"You were gone for a lot more than ten minutes."

"I was only planning to stop at the crafts store to run in and get one thing, Cooper, something that I needed for Carly's *Hansel and Gretel* set. I wasn't out shopping for myself. It didn't seem worth dragging Carly along with me when I was only going for such a short time to a store half a mile away. But then on the way home, I felt sleepy. I was up late last night, working on my quilt."

And the night before that. My bedroom was next to her studio, and I'd heard her sewing machine whirring all night long.

"So I pulled over and took a short nap, which is the sensible and safe thing to do. Would you rather I fell asleep at the wheel?"

"I was just worried, that's all." I hesitated. "Maybe you should sleep more at night."

She gave a laugh. "Says the boy who probably isn't

going to sleep for ten minutes tonight at Spencer's sleep-over. Speaking of which, why are you here?"

"Carly called me. She was scared being at home alone."

"Carly, honey," Mom said, gathering Carly into a hug. "There was nothing to be scared of. I was coming right back."

But you didn't come right back, I wanted to say.

"I'm here now, Coop, so why don't you head on over to Spencer's?"

"I already had the pizza and cake." Well, the pizza. Not the cake. "So I think I'll just stay here." I didn't want to leave Carly, in case Mom disappeared again.

Up in my room, I turned on my computer and Googled "doesn't sleep." The screen filled with posts by parents who were trying to get their babies to sleep through the night. I Googled "too many projects" and retrieved a screen full of articles on time management. Spencer and I used to try typing in all kinds of weird things like "you are stupid" and "big fat loser," just to see what would come up. So now I Googled "My mom has changed." But I didn't find any Web site that told me why she had changed, or what I could do about it.

11

Thanksgiving was coming, and in Food Fun, Mr. Pasta taught us how to make a piecrust. He started by explaining that it couldn't be explained.

"You can read a dozen books on how to make piecrust; there are entire Web sites devoted to the art of making piecrust; a master chef can show you his secrets. But none of this will be of the slightest use unless you can *feel* it in your fingers."

Spencer spread out his hands on the table, fingers splayed. "I don't think my fingers are going to be good at feeling piecrust," he predicted gloomily.

"There are four ingredients for any piecrust," Mr. Pasta continued. "Flour, salt, liquid, and fat."

"Why is everyone looking at me?" Spencer asked, although nobody was. He gave a protective pat to his chubby midsection. I returned Ben's grin. It was good to be with normal people, people who all thought the same things were funny.

The best kind of fat for piecrust, according to

Mr. Pasta, was lard. The word *lard* alone was enough to send half the class into giggles. The second best was butter. That was what the class was going to use for their pies. Mr. Pasta didn't want to hear the words *margarine* or *Crisco* mentioned in his presence. I made a mental note to strike those words from my vocabulary, not that I had ever uttered the word *Crisco* in my entire life.

"It is crucial," Mr. Pasta intoned, "that the fat be very cold."

"Cold fat," Spencer remarked. "How appealing."

"When you combine the fat with the flour, you do not want to blend them. You just want to cover the fat particles with flour. Your flour-covered fat lumps should be no larger than peas."

"Pea-size fat lumps," Spencer echoed. "Yum!"

Mr. Pasta gave a warning look to our station. Ben poked Spencer to be quiet.

"Ow!" Spencer exclaimed, but he dropped his voice to a whisper. "How would you like it if I poked *you* in *your* fat lump?"

Even Ben had difficulty when it was time to roll out our piecrust. It kept sticking to the counter, and to the rolling pin. First it wasn't rolled out thin enough, and then it was rolled out so thin that it tore when Ben tried to lift it to place it in the pie pan.

Lindsay's table was evidently having just as much trouble. She came over to our table to compare notes.

"Ours must have some glue in it or something. It won't stop sticking," Lindsay complained with a grin.

I couldn't think of anything clever to reply. "Ours keeps sticking, too."

"At least you got yours in the pie plate."

"Ben did it." I wished I was good at everything like Ben, or funny like Spencer. Then again, Lindsay had plainly come to our table to talk to me and not to them.

"We forgot to take Peter Pepper home with us," Lindsay said. "I didn't remember him until after my mom was pulling into the garage."

"I didn't remember him, either."

"I wonder if he misses us," Lindsay said.

"I bet he does. He was a good, faithful pepper."

"Lindsay!" one of her table mates called to her. "You're missing out on the total destruction and ruination of the world's worst piecrust!"

"Gotta go," Lindsay said.

"Sure," I said.

The last two minutes had been the best two minutes I had had in weeks.

That day after lunch, outside on the blacktop, I wandered over to where Mr. Stuart was standing on outdoor duty. I wanted to talk to somebody about Mom, and Mr. Stuart was my favorite teacher, not counting Mr. Pasta, whose expertise focused on cooking, baking, and eating.

"Hey, Cooper." Mr. Stuart laid a friendly hand on my shoulder. "How's it going?"

I wanted to tell him about how strange Mom had acted at the Community Table, and how she had left

Carly alone while she went out shopping, and how the answering machine tape at our house these days was filled with phone calls from credit card companies and long, rambling messages from some homeless man who wanted to be part of Mom's art show.

Instead I said, "It's okay."

There was an awkward silence. "Okay" was a stupid answer to give if I wanted my teacher to ask me what was wrong.

"Anything on your mind?"

"No." "No" was even stupider.

"Are you sure?"

"Yeah." I couldn't talk to him about Mom, I just couldn't. "It's all okay."

I picked up a basketball that had rolled toward my feet and threw it back to the guys playing hoops, and that was the end of the conversation with Mr. Stuart.

For the rest of the afternoon I thought about trying to talk to Ben's mom, or Spencer's. But Ben's mom was so perfect; I didn't want her to know how not-perfect our family was. And Spencer's mom was so loud; I could imagine her shouting at me, "*What?* Your mom did *what?*" Besides, what if I said something to them about my mom and then they went and talked to her? I mean, the whole point of talking to them would be so that they would go talk to her. And then she'd know that it had all come from me, that I had been the one who had told them, and it would all be so hideous I didn't think I could stand it.

If only Mom's doctor would see that there was something wrong and do something about it. But at home that afternoon, when I checked the calendar, there were no more appointments written there, and I didn't see the bottle of pills next to her bed. Maybe she had stopped taking them, and that's why she was acting so weird.

What if *I* tried to talk to her about it? I practiced the first line in my head: "Mom, I think— Mom, you're acting strange." Could I actually say it? But Mom had left to run errands, and I had no idea when she'd be back.

While I waited for her to return, I started trying to clean up the kitchen. Instead of complaining about how messy the house was, maybe I could make things better. If the house looked less crazy, it might make her be less crazy, too.

I started with the table. Dirty dishes I rinsed and put into the dishwasher, not that rinsing did anything to dissolve the dried-on, caked-on food residue from days —or weeks?—ago. Yellowing newspapers went into the recycling bin in the garage. I knew Mom wasn't going to get around to framing Carly's artwork anytime soon, so I organized it into a neat stack and set it on top of the refrigerator, out of the way. The bolts of fabric I lugged up to her studio. Even if there was no room for it there, it was better to have fabric in a quilting studio than on a kitchen table. The heaps of unpaid bills I put on the counter: maybe she'd be more likely to pay them if she could actually see them. When I reached the scraps of fabric and gold braid from the toy soldier costumes, I threw them in the kitchen trash, and then carried the trash out to the bin.

I had never seen a sight more lovely than the bare expanse of uncluttered tablecloth I finally uncovered. I took the tablecloth outside to shake off a few lingering crumbs, then smoothed it back in place, carefully positioning the salt and pepper shakers in the middle.

It looked like the kitchen table at Ben's house.

It looked exactly like a normal mother's kitchen table.

When Mom walked in from the garage half an hour later, I was standing by the table, unable to keep myself from grinning with pride. In the poem "Jabberwocky," one of Mom's favorites, there was a line about someone "chortling" with joy. I now knew exactly what it felt like to chortle.

She was about to deposit her shopping bag unthinkingly on the table when she did a double take.

"Cooper!"

"I cleaned it up."

I waited for her praise.

"What did you do with my things? My fabric? Carly's artwork? Did you throw them away?"

"I *put* them away."

"Where? You had no right! Cooper, I had all this organized, and then you just swoop in and move everything willy-nilly, so now I can't find it?"

Organized? Dirty dishes next to old newspapers next to unpaid bills next to unframed artwork next to quilting fabric next to scraps of gold braid from toy soldier costumes made a month ago?

"I thought you'd be happy! I was trying to help!"

"When I need help around here, I'll ask you for it."

I wanted to ask her whether she was still seeing Dr. Leibowitz. I wanted to tell her how worried I was. But I couldn't find the words. Instead, I went upstairs and practiced my trombone, good and loud, for half an hour.

By suppertime, she had the table strewed with the results of her afternoon's shopping—more fabric—and the contents of the crisper from the refrigerator: limp carrots, soggy lettuce, bruised onions, and a moldy piece of ginger root.

It was as if my whole hour of cleaning had never happened.

12

Usually, Gran-Dan didn't come to Colorado for Thanksgiving, and we didn't go to New Jersey. The holiday airfares were too high, and the holiday crowds were too large. For the past several years, we had spent the day with Jodie's family, each family alternating turns as host. If only this year were the year to go to Jodie's house! But it wasn't.

"We need to start cleaning up the house," I told my mom on Monday morning. Carly and I had the whole week off from school.

"Well, go ahead and run the vacuum," Mom said.

I stared at the living room carpet, entirely covered with her piles of fabric.

"Just vacuum around them."

"I could carry them upstairs to your studio."

"After I've spent weeks laying them out exactly in this way to get a feel for the color?"

"But it's just three days until Thanksgiving."

"Three days," she repeated, making it sound as if three days was the same as three years.

The day before Thanksgiving, the house looked just the same, if not worse, and while Mom had done some of the other shopping, she hadn't yet bought the turkey. She liked to get a fresh turkey, not a frozen one, and there was no room in the refrigerator to put it, so she was waiting until the last minute.

"What if they run out of turkeys?" I asked her.

"O ye of little faith," she replied.

I spent the afternoon baking a pumpkin pie, with an awestruck Carly as my audience, but I cheated and used a frozen piecrust. If even Ben couldn't make a successful piecrust with Mr. Pasta standing three feet away, I wasn't going to risk trying it without assistance.

Carly and I went with Mom after supper when she finally decided it was time to go to King Soopers and buy the turkey; her favorite organic food store, where she usually bought her free-range turkeys, was already closed for the day.

"Keep your fingers crossed," she told us as we parked in the mostly deserted lot.

I crossed them, but it didn't help. The refrigerator bin in the meat department where the turkeys had been was empty. We even checked the freezer: no turkeys there, either.

"Excuse me," Mom asked one of the store clerks. "Might you have any turkeys in the back? Could you check for us?"

"Nope," the man said. "I mean, I wouldn't mind checking, but I know already what I'd find. Nothing. Nada. Zip. You're the third person who's come in tonight asking. And we ordered fifty more turkeys than we did last year."

"What are we going to do?" I asked, once the man headed off to the deli counter.

"Jodie's family is coming," Carly added, as if contributing some new fact to the discussion.

"We should have bought it sooner," I couldn't resist saying, though I made sure to say "we" instead of "you."

Mom's eyes flared. "How was I supposed to know that King Soopers wasn't going to order the right amount? You'd think that a major supermarket chain wouldn't be surprised that their customers want to buy a *turkey* for *Thanksgiving* and would plan accordingly."

"We could have chicken," I suggested. We could be the only family in America having chicken for Thanksgiving.

"Close enough!" Mom said. She found a roasting chicken and put it in the cart.

"It won't be the same," Carly said, her voice wobbling a little bit.

"Maybe we can buy a big cardboard turkey," Mom said. "You know, one of those ones that fan out and fasten around. At least we'd have some kind of turkey on the table. Let's go look at the holiday aisle."

She was laughing now. "Look at it this way: Thanksgiving is always the same old same old. This will be the different Thanksgiving, the Thanksgiving without a turkey. The side dishes are always the best part anyway, the stuffing, and the creamed onions, and the pumpkin pie. And this year we'll have Chef Cooper's special pumpkin pie."

The holiday aisle was freshly stocked with Christmas decorations—long rolls of wrapping paper, boxes of shiny red, green, and gold ornaments, plush snowmen and Santas. In the Thanksgiving section, the shelves were almost bare. I picked up the one remaining turkey, a three-inch-tall wax candle. The turkey's comb had partly melted and run down over one eye.

Mom gave another laugh. "He's better than nothing, don't you think? He looks like he could use a good home."

I forced a laugh in return, but I wondered: was our house really a good home? For a wax candle turkey, not to mention for me and Carly?

Jodie's family was coming at five; at four o'clock the house still looked terrible, though it smelled appealingly of the chicken and stuffing baking in the oven. Finally, at four-thirty, Mom started carrying armloads of fabric upstairs, directing Carly and me to help her. I frantically ran the vacuum over the most visible areas of the newly exposed carpet, and Carly darted around with a dustcloth. Then came the mad scramble to set the table.

"We'll turn the lights down low, and it will look fine," Mom said. "We'll eat by candlelight. It will be our turkey candle's finest moment."

When Jodie's family arrived promptly at five, the house was acceptable. Mom explained to them that this was going to be the Thanksgiving with chicken rather than turkey, presenting it as a hilariously funny story about the terrible lack of planning at King Soopers. At least Jodie's parents both chuckled.

"The side dishes are always the best part anyway," Jodie's mother said, just as Mom had said the day before.

But everyone knew that the best part was the turkey.

"And, anyway, we do have a turkey!" Mom said gaily. "Carly, run and get him. You know, our little wax turkey friend from the table!"

At just that moment, the lights went out.

Mom was laughing so hard now she could hardly speak. Jodie's parents weren't laughing; they were smiling in a sort of awkward, embarrassed way.

"No . . . turkey! And no . . . electricity!" Mom gasped between spasms of laughter. "Well, the Pilgrims didn't have electricity, either, on their first Thanksgiving."

They had a turkey, though.

"I wonder how extensive a blackout this is." Jodie's father walked over to the window to survey the state of the rest of the neighborhood. Joining him, I could see that everybody else's lights were on, including the porch light next door at Jodie's house.

"Hmm," Jodie's father said. "It looks like it's just your house, Emily. Maybe your oven blew a fuse? Where's your fuse box? Let me take a look."

When he checked, he found that it wasn't a blown fuse.

"Maybe the utility company has it in for you, Em," Jodie's father teased. "What did you do to tick them off? Late on your bills?"

He obviously meant it as a joke, but I thought of the unopened bills on the kitchen counter.

The six of us ended up carrying what there was of the Thanksgiving feast over to Jodie's house and eating it there. Even without company expected, Jodie's house was clean and orderly, the dining room table decorated with a centerpiece of a cornucopia and autumn leaves.

The wax candle turkey came with us: my mom insisted. "It's his special day!"

We didn't light his wick. He just stood on the table, the table without a turkey, next door to the house without electricity.

"Let's go around the table and each say what we're grateful for," Jodie's mother instructed.

"I'm grateful that I'm friends with Jodie," Carly said.

"I'm grateful that I'm friends with Carly," Jodie said.

"I'm grateful that my depression is behind me, and I'm finally well again!" Mom said.

Jodie's mother took Mom's hand. "Yes, thank God for that," she said, but I thought she looked worried.

I still didn't know what I was going to say when it was my turn. I was grateful that Thanksgiving was almost over, grateful that it hadn't turned out even worse, grateful that my pie looked so pretty on the sideboard, with the edges of the crust crimped so evenly and golden brown.

"Cooper?" Jodie's mother prompted.

"I'm grateful that I know how to bake a pie." I hoped it came out funny, the way Spencer would have said it, and it must have sounded funny enough, because everybody laughed.

Later, when dinner was done and everybody was mostly finished cleaning up, I was heading back to the kitchen to get one last sliver of leftover pie to snack on while I watched some football with Jodie's dad; Jodie and Carly were up in Jodie's room playing.

At the kitchen door, I overheard my mom and Jodie's mom, Jodie's mom's voice so low I couldn't make out what she was saying, my mom's voice too loud, as it always was these days.

"Of course I'm unusually energetic! Sally, I did nothing but lie in bed all summer long! I have so much lost time to make up for!"

Jodie's mom murmured something else.

Then my mom: "No, I'm not seeing Dr. Leibowitz anymore. I don't need to see her. You go to a doctor when you're sick, not when you're well."

Then: "I appreciate your concern, Sally, really I do, but I've never felt better in my entire life!"

I slipped back to the football game without my pie. I couldn't have swallowed it anyway. A grownup had finally talked to Mom, and what had it accomplished?

Absolutely nothing.

Nothing at all.

The lights were back on by Friday afternoon; apparently Mom had found the money somewhere to pay the electric bill. I spent the rest of Thanksgiving break mostly at Ben's or Spencer's; Carly spent most of it with Jodie. The few hours that we were home we spent together in Inchland.

Before, I had listened as Carly made up the Inchland stories. But lately she was so quiet that I was doing most of the talking.

"I'm surprised that King Inchard and Queen Incharina aren't more worried about Princess Inchitella," I said. "I mean, she's their only child, and a princess of royal blood, and she's been gone for ages. And let's face it, it's not like Inchland is a big country."

"I don't think they ever really loved her," Carly said. "They were always too busy with their royal activities to spend any time with her. That's why she left, remember? Because she was so lonely."

"She's not lonely now." I tried to sound positive and encouraging. "Now she has Parsley. But, hey, maybe the two of them get lonely sometimes, too. Or bored, just hanging out together. Do you think they need a pet?"

We had had a dog named Muffy, but Muffy had died two years ago, and we hadn't had the heart to replace him.

"Maybe."

Carly didn't say anything else, so I went on with the story. "One day, when Inchitella and Parsley are out walking around Inchland, they see a tiny kitten, just six weeks old. Its mother had an accident—she was run over by a car."

"Cooper! You know they don't have cars in Inchland."

"I meant by a carriage. Inchitella and Parsley hear the kitten crying, so Inchitella picks it up and warms it in her cloak, and they carry it home to the stable and feed it warm milk. And then they name it . . . What would be a good name for a kitten?"

When Carly didn't offer any suggestions, I said, "Button. So that's how Button came to live with Inchitella and Parsley. Did you know that Button has magical powers?"

Carly shook her head. I thought she was starting to look more interested.

"Yes. Button is very small, of course, like everything else in Inchland, but Button can turn herself big when she wants to, so that Parsley and Inchitella can ride on her back."

"Does she crush the buildings when she walks?"

"No. You know how cats are. She places her paws very carefully."

"Are the other Inchies afraid when they see her?"

"No, they can't see her, because when she turns herself big she turns herself invisible, too."

"Where does Button sleep?" Carly asked.

"In a basket. A straw basket lined with down from Inchland ducklings."

"I have a little doll's hat made of straw!" Carly remembered. "We can use it for Button's basket."

In an instant she had found it in her closet. Turned upside down, and lined with a few snippets of yarn, it was the perfect bed for a tiny stray kitten.

"Inchitella and Parsley have a special song they sing to Button when they want her to go to sleep," I continued. I didn't like to have anybody hear me sing, even Carly, so I just said the words aloud as I made them up. "Sleep, little Button, curl up and rest. Sleep, little Button, safe in your nest."

"Say it again," Carly begged.

I did. Then Carly sang it, to a tune of her own, in her high, pure voice. The song wasn't a sad song—what was sad about a simple lullaby?—but Button was so safe and snug in her basket, and it had been so long since I had felt that way, that I had to look down so that Carly wouldn't see how close I was to crying.

13

As the date of the first and only performance of *Hansel and Gretel* approached, I knew Carly's lines as well as she did from hearing her recite them so often.

"Look, Hansel! It's a house! A house made out of gingerbread, all covered with candy!"

"Oh, Hansel! The old witch has put you in this cage because she means to eat you!"

"I am only a stupid little girl, Old Mother. I do not know how to peek into the oven. Please show me."

But as far as I could tell, Mom had made no progress on constructing the house, the cage, or the oven. She wasn't working on her quilt for the quilt show, either. To my relief, she also seemed to have forgotten about Inchland, though a half-finished, teensy-weensy tea set, fashioned of modeling clay, sat on the kitchen counter, in danger of being crushed by the gigantic, human-size dirty dishes that towered over it. Instead, she had thrown her energies into planning a family vacation.

"Where should we go for winter break?" she asked Carly and me one night at dinner.

"New Jersey," Carly said promptly. "To see Gran-Dan."

Talk about a bad idea. What would Gran-Dan do if Mom were let loose in his neat, orderly house, strewing her stuff all over it, spreading chaos everywhere? We'd spend the whole break doing nothing but listening to the two of them fight.

"We go there all the time," Mom said. "This year we need to go somewhere special. There's a whole big world out there for us to see." Her face lit up. "Wait!"

She hopped up from the table and headed upstairs. In a moment she had returned with a long roll of plain white paper and a box of markers. "We'll make a list of all our ideas. Carly, you go first. Think of someplace exciting."

"Alaska?" Carly suggested. "Or Hawaii? Because we're studying them this year in school?"

Mom had already cut a four-foot length of paper from the roll and taped it to the side of the kitchen cabinets. ALASKA, she wrote, in large blue letters on the top of the paper, and then beneath it, in green letters, HAWAII.

"Cooper?"

"Hawaii would be pretty cool." I wouldn't mind a long white beach beside the sparkling blue ocean, bordered with palm trees.

"Carly already said Hawaii. Think of somewhere different. Paris! London!"

"Don't we need passports to go to Europe?"

Mom waved her hand. "I found a site on the Internet where you can get passports in forty-eight hours."

"Okay, Paris," I said, since I obviously had to say something.

She wrote PARIS on the list in alternating red and blue letters.

"Where do *you* want to go?" Carly asked.

For answer Mom flashed us a grin and continued adding to the list: PERU, PATAGONIA, EGYPT, NIGERIA, NEW ZEALAND, INDONESIA, BRAZIL.

By the time she finally laid down her marker, I thought that the only place not on the list was the only place I really wanted to go: Inchland.

At school, I got the second-highest grade on a math test, which was a pleasant surprise. Mrs. Alpert was home recovering from surgery; our substitute for Language Arts didn't care whether we put our names on the top left-hand corner, top right-hand corner, or even at the bottom of the page. Poached Egg had us playing basketball, on enormous teams with twenty kids on a side. In social studies we were doing current events. You got extra credit if you could find newspaper articles about Mexico, Central America, or South America. I found one on the destruction of the rain forests in Brazil.

Mr. Pasta's class was gearing up for "Pasta Live," the cooking show scheduled for the same week as Carly's play. The "Pasta Live" show was planned in two parts.

In the first half, teams of students would demonstrate cooking techniques and produce a bunch of snacks that the audience could enjoy at intermission. In the second half, Mr. Pasta would take the stage, wearing his chef's hat and waving his spatula, in competition with a trio of parent challengers.

I was exceedingly grateful that my mother was not one of them. Two dads had already come forward, plus Ben's mom, who was a wonderful cook. I had conveniently "forgotten" to bring home the notice with the call for volunteers. With any luck, my mom might miss the show altogether, because she would be busy working on the set for Carly's play the next day.

Six students were going to be onstage during the second half serving as chefs' assistants, three helping the parent team and three helping Mr. Pasta. For fairness, Mr. Pasta drew the names out of a hat. I was surprised when mine was the second name chosen for the parent team. Even in a lottery, I had somehow expected Ben to be the one picked. Lindsay's name was the third name drawn for Mr. Pasta's team. It was too bad the two of us weren't on the same team, in case there were going to be any peppers that needed chopping.

When Gran-Dan called that weekend, I told him about "Pasta Live." I didn't say anything more to him about Thanksgiving. The week before, I had overheard Mom telling him about the turkey, and the power failure, but of course she made it sound like the funniest story ever.

"So there's going to be a contest between Mr. Pasta, I mean Mr. Costa, and three of the parents."

"Is your mom one of them? She sure seems to be going like gangbusters these days, talking a mile a minute and quilting up a storm from what she tells me."

It was the perfect chance for me to say something. I sometimes wonder what would have happened if I had told Gran-Dan then, about the credit card bills, and the power outage, and the way she laughed too loud, and the unbelievable mess everywhere. But Gran-Dan kept on talking.

"Quilting is well and good, I told her, but it doesn't pay the bills, and your dad's Social Security survivor benefits only stretch so far. My advice, Cooper, is pay the bills first and keep the artsy stuff as a hobby."

I couldn't imagine my mom with her quilting as a hobby, doing some boring job all day long that she'd hate.

"I don't do any artsy stuff," I lied. "Carly's the artsy one."

"Well, the two of you go at it together most of the time, it seems to me," Gran-Dan said. He made it sound like a criticism. "Pirates. Igloos."

It was a good thing he didn't know about Inchland, even though it was his deeds that had started it all.

"Go ahead and put Carly on the phone, will you?" he said then.

"I'll go look for her," I said. And our conversation was over.

14

To my great relief, on Sunday a plywood structure began taking shape in the living room. The witch's gingerbread house had a slanting roof rising to a pointy peak. The door of the house was going to be a real door that opened and shut, so that Hansel, Gretel, and the witch could go in and out. On each side of the door, Mom had planned a shuttered window, with a window box abloom with red and yellow wooden lollipops.

Carly and I helped to paint the lollipops at the kitchen table Monday after school. "Pasta Live" was going to be on Tuesday evening; Carly's play, on Wednesday.

"We only need to paint the fronts," I said. "No one's going to be able to see the backs."

"God will," Mom commented. Then she explained, "When Michelangelo painted the Sistine Chapel ceiling, he spent just as much time on the parts no one in the chapel would ever be able to see, because God would be seeing them."

Good for Michelangelo, I wanted to say. Or *Do you re-ally think God cares about the backs of lollipops for a second-grade play?* Instead I asked, "How long did it take him to paint it? The whole ceiling?"

"Four years."

I hoped Mom would notice that we didn't have four years to make the set for *Hansel and Gretel.* We had two days, and one of those days would be taken up with the cooking show at Western Hills.

"Have you started making the oven yet? And Hansel's cage?" I asked.

Mom looked annoyed. "No, I haven't started making the oven yet. Or Hansel's cage. Maybe you haven't noticed that I'm already working twenty hours a day on building the house, and trying to find budget airfares for winter break, and applying for our passports, not to mention finishing my quilt, and sending in the grant application for the art show at the Community Table. I can't do everything, Cooper!"

"Cooper and I can finish painting the lollipops," Carly offered. "We just need five more red ones and five more yellow ones. We can do them while you start on the oven and the cage."

"Will you two stop talking about that oven and cage?" Mom's voice had a hard, angry edge to it. "I know what needs to get done. I know how long it takes to do it. I don't need my own children reminding me."

She snatched at the jar of yellow tempera paint just as Carly reached for it to paint her next yellow lollipop.

I watched in silent horror as the jar tipped over, its bright paint racing across the table like a wave rushing onto the Jersey shore, surging past the edge of the table to cascade in a flat waterfall onto the kitchen floor.

"Don't just sit there!" Mom shouted. "Cooper! Carly! *Do* something!"

I jumped up and ran to grab a roll of paper towels from the dispenser by the sink. The dispenser was empty. Mom flung a terry-cloth dish towel onto the floor. It lay half drowned in the spreading yellow pool.

"See what you did?" she accused Carly. "The towel is ruined now, *and* the floor, *and* the tabletop. And you're yelling at *me* about making you an *oven*?"

Carly burst into tears. "I didn't mean to, I didn't, I was just trying to help!"

"I don't need this kind of help! I don't need any help from either of you!"

"Fine!" I found my voice. "We won't help. Come on, Carly, let's go upstairs."

"Go, then! Leave me with all of your mess to clean up."

Still sobbing, Carly followed me out of the kitchen. I didn't know what Mom would do when she saw the yellow footprints trailing across the living room carpet behind us.

Upstairs in my room, I did my math homework and practiced trombone, trying not to feel guilty for leaving Carly alone. Once I was calmer, I looked in on her, glad to see her busy at her little table. "What are you drawing?"

"Button. Cooper, do you think Button could be a bunny and not a kitten? She seems more like a bunny to me."

"Sure."

I sat down in the second chair at Carly's low table and reached for a sheet of blank paper.

"What are you going to draw?" she asked.

"I'll draw Button, too, with Inchitella and Parsley flying on her back."

"You didn't tell me Button could fly! I thought they rode on her like a horse."

"They fly on her like a flying horse."

"Does she have wings?"

I thought for a minute. I somehow couldn't imagine a winged rabbit. "She flies without wings."

"Where do they go?"

"Wherever they want to go. They fly over other countries, but all the other countries are too big. The people are like giants—bigger than giants, monsters. And the cars and the buses—they're like humongous dragons. So they always fly back to Inchland, where everything is the right size."

"Cooper?"

"Uh-huh?"

"Is it okay that I told Mom about Inchland?"

No, it isn't okay. I shrugged. "I don't think anything can happen to Inchland. Because it's magic."

"I put the deeds in my treasure box, all eight of them, yours and mine. It locks, you know. I hid the key. Should I tell you where I hid it?"

"You don't have to tell me."

"I want to. It's in the stable, under the mattress on Parsley's bed. I figure Parsley would be good at protecting it while we're away on our trip for winter break."

"I don't think we're going away after all."

"That's okay. Inchitella and Parsley would miss us if we went, don't you think?"

"Yeah," I agreed. "I think they would."

I arrived at school for "Pasta Live" at six o'clock on Tuesday evening; Spencer's mom drove us. Two food stations had been set up on the stage in the auditorium, with a stove, fridge, microwave, and counter at each one, but no sink.

For the first half, our team had been assigned the task of preparing what Mr. Pasta called "crudités"—a fancy word for "veggies and dip." We had already arranged that Ben would do all of the talking into the microphone, and most of the chopping as well. Other groups were preparing mini-sandwiches, barbecued meatballs, chips and homemade salsa, and a warm artichoke and cheese dip, served with slices of crusty French bread. Lindsay's team was making the punch, with frozen strawberries floating on top.

The show began at six-thirty. Mr. Pasta came forward to the microphone. "Welcome, parents, siblings, teachers, friends, and all lovers of fine food! Tonight we invite you to embark with us on a culinary adventure." It was dark enough in the auditorium that I couldn't see whether Mom and Carly were there. I said a quick prayer that they hadn't come.

First up was the meatball-making team. They managed to get their meatballs into their Crock-Pot in a timely way. Only one meatball landed on the floor, and Mr. Pasta intervened just before the student who dropped it was about to pick it up and plop it back into the pot.

The salsa makers didn't spill or drop anything, but their spokesperson spoke so quickly and softly that no one could hear what she said, even with the microphone. The teams were taking turns passing around a clip-on mike so we could have our hands free for the demonstrations.

"Next, Ben, Spencer, and Cooper will show us how to prepare crudités," Mr. Pasta announced. He pronounced it "croo-dih-tay," rolling the *r* in an exaggerated French way.

"Crudités are healthy and easy to prepare," Ben said. "Our team will be serving celery, peppers, and baby carrots, together with a fresh dill and yogurt dip."

Deftly, Ben began cutting the celery stalks into small spears. I took charge of cutting up the red, green, and yellow peppers, since peppers now held a special place in my heart. I hoped that Lindsay, seated on the stage with her team, noticed. Spencer, ever the ham, did a short comic routine in which he engaged in elaborate preparations for cutting up the baby carrots with a flourish of his large knife but then just dumped the already bite-size carrots onto the serving tray. Some chuckles came from the audience. Ben stirred together the dill weed and plain yogurt, and we were done.

At intermission, all the teams carried their offerings into the large open area outside the auditorium. Across the crowd, I saw Carly and Mom. Reluctantly, I went over to join them.

"I want to take Food Fun when I'm in sixth grade!" Carly said. "I want to make the punch with the strawberries."

"Where's Mr. Costa?" Mom asked. For a moment I wasn't sure who she was talking about; I had almost forgotten Mr. Pasta's real name. "I want to ask him if I could hire your class to cater the reception for the opening of the homeless shelter art show."

"No," I said, before I had a chance to realize how it would sound.

"No, what?"

"He's not going to want us to do that. He has too many other things planned."

"Well, there's no harm in asking, is there? That's him over there, isn't it? I'll be right back."

Say no, say no, say no. I beamed the words in Mr. Pasta's direction. But as Mom approached him, Mr. Pasta tapped on a glass with a spoon to get everybody's attention. The rest of the crowd was drinking punch out of paper cups, but leave it to Mr. Pasta to be drinking his out of a real glass, and eating his snacks on a proper plate.

"Excuse me, ladies and gentlemen. I trust you are all enjoying the delectable tidbits prepared for us by our fine young chefs!"

The families applauded loudly in response.

"It has come to my attention that unfortunately one of our three parent challengers had to offer his regrets for the second half of the evening. Illness has kept him at home tonight. I know this is short notice, but is there anyone here who would be willing to take his place?"

Instantly Mom had her hand in the air. I never found out if any other parents would have volunteered, because of course Mr. Pasta spied her right away, given that she was standing not two feet in front of him.

"Bravo!" He clapped her appreciatively on the back. "I admire your courage!"

My heart clenched like a fist. I felt as if most of the oxygen had been suddenly sucked out of the room.

15

We have to stop her," I said to Carly.

Carly tugged at my sleeve. "I don't understand. What is Mom going to do?"

I wished I knew, or maybe it was better not to know. "It's going to be like one of those cooking shows on TV," I told Carly. "Each side—the three parents on one side, and Mr. Pasta on the other side—will get a bunch of ingredients, and they'll have half an hour to make something out of them. Then the judges—he has some eighth graders and their parents for the judges—will eat both things and decide which side is the winner."

"Mom's a good cook," Carly said loyally. "I hope Mom wins!"

I just hoped I could live through the next hour.

Back in the auditorium, I hurried up onstage to join the chefs' assistants for the parents' team, wishing I could be sitting on the floor in front of the stage with Ben and Spencer and the other kids from our class. Mr. Stuart came to the microphone to serve as the emcee for the second half of the show, since Mr. Pasta would be busy cooking.

Mr. Stuart read out the list of ingredients: boneless chicken breasts, sun-dried tomatoes, goat cheese, and half a dozen other things. I hardly listened, torn between wanting to keep my eyes on my mother every single second and wanting to keep them shut until it was all over. I hoped I'd get an easy task so I wouldn't mess it up in front of everybody.

The teams had five minutes to plan, while the eighth-grade judges wheeled out rolling trays laden with the needed supplies. The three members of the parent team conferred with one another; Mr. Pasta, grinning broadly, conferred with himself. Standing a little bit to the side, I could hear my mother's voice, louder than the others: "Presentation! I'm an artist, so I'll take care of the presentation."

Presentation, I knew from Mr. Pasta, was how the food looked on the plate, how it was *presented* to the diners. I greatly doubted that the eighth-grade judges would care about presentation. But maybe their parents would be impressed.

As the teams began cooking, Ben's mother gave me the job of dicing celery and onions. At least I could do it without thinking. Mr. Stuart went back and forth between the two teams, offering each the chance to speak into the handheld microphone, sharing their plans and techniques with the audience. When it was the parent team's turn, he held out the mike to Ben's mom, but my mom intercepted it. I wondered if Mr. Stuart would recognize her as my mom. Probably not: he talked to so many parents during the course of a year, and it was a coincidence that both my mom and I had ended up onstage together.

"We're grilling our chicken breasts—Brad is grilling them—while Michelle prepares a topping of crumbled goat cheese and sun-dried tomatoes. I'm working on dessert—leave it to me to go for the dessert!" She laughed too loudly, given that what she had said wasn't all that funny. The audience obligingly returned her laughter.

"How does this sound? Fresh raspberries, drizzled with melted dark chocolate, topped with whipped cream and a few shavings of the chocolate?"

She moaned appreciatively, as if she were overcome, almost fainting, with pleasure. I felt my cheeks flushing with embarrassment.

"They don't sound that good," I heard Brad whisper to Michelle.

No kidding.

"Let me go check on how Mr. Costa is doing," Mr. Stuart said.

Mom didn't relinquish the microphone. "We already know how Mr. Costa is doing," she said. "He's losing! Because the three of us—Brad, Michelle, and Emily—can't be beat!"

She turned to the audience, as if expecting them to go wild for the parent team. A few parents clapped in response, apparently thinking that was what they were supposed to be doing, but when the other parents didn't join in, the feeble applause died out. My mom didn't seem to notice.

"The parents—united—will never be—defeated!" she chanted. No one else took up the chant.

Mr. Stuart reached out his hand and took the microphone away from her. I half expected her to engage in a tussle with him to keep it, but fortunately she didn't.

"All right," Mr. Stuart said pleasantly. "We've heard from the parent team. Now let's see what Mr. Costa is cooking up for us."

Mr. Pasta announced that he was stuffing his chicken breasts with the goat cheese and the sun-dried tomatoes and then baking them in a 400-degree oven for twenty minutes. For dessert he was making a raspberry chocolate mousse.

"Go, Mr. Pasta!" one of the sixth graders called out, and a bunch of the kids started stomping their feet and whistling, which made me feel better. Maybe this was how a cooking competition was supposed to be, with the parents cheering on the parents, and the students cheering on their teacher. Maybe my mom had just been trying to get everybody into the spirit of the thing.

"Go, parents!" someone else shouted.

I felt even better.

My mother clasped her upraised hands and swung them from side to side in the air, like a heavyweight boxing champ.

I felt worse.

In his second stop to chat with the parent team, Mr. Stuart managed to give the mike to Ben's mom, who made some brief, appropriate remarks. As the clock continued ticking, Mr. Pasta whisked his chicken breasts into the oven and was assembling a salad of greens, raspberries, and walnuts.

Onions and celery all neatly chopped, I didn't have anything left to do, so I stood, as hidden as possible, behind the parent team, watching as Mom whipped the cream with an electric mixer. Across the stage, Lindsay looked busy chopping walnuts for Mr. Pasta, so I couldn't catch her eye to smile. Not that I felt like smiling. In another ten minutes, the whistle would blow, signaling the end of the cook-off. I only had to get through ten more agonizing minutes.

On Mr. Stuart's third visit to their cooking station, Mom pounced on the microphone again and oohed and aahed over the sizzling golden-brown chicken breasts coming off the grill and the pungent aroma of the cheese and tomato topping. She made a special fuss, of course, over her own snowy peaks of whipped cream.

"Mom," I hissed desperately behind her. Couldn't she see the huge clock hung on the side of the stage? "There's just three minutes left!"

I couldn't tell if she had heard me or not; I had tried to keep my voice low enough that no one else would hear.

"Mom!" I whispered again, louder this time. Finally, she surrendered the mike back to Mr. Stuart.

Her other team members had already started to assemble the plates of chicken to serve to the judges.

"I told you I was going to do the presentation!" she said, her voice rising in irritation. I hoped the people in the audience couldn't hear her.

"We can handle them," Ben's mother said, with Ben's same unruffled calm. "You need to take care of that fabulous dessert! Is the chocolate melted?"

"How could I be melting the chocolate when I was busy whipping the cream?" Mom snatched the unwrapped bar of solid chocolate, dumped it into a glass bowl, and slammed it in the microwave. As she whirled back to the counter, her elbow caught the glass bowl of whipped cream.

I leaped to catch it, but I was too far away. The bowl went crashing onto the floor, shattering into pieces. She gave a desperate cry. Frantic, I wondered if I could scoop any of the spilled whipped cream into another container as she knelt down to start grabbing up the foam-covered pieces of broken glass.

Then I heard cheers. Prepared for the fun of food messes from years of eating in the school cafeteria, the sixth-grade audience had burst into raucous applause, almost drowning out the sound of Mr. Stuart's whistle.

"Time!" Mr. Stuart called out above the din.

Scarier than the witch in *Hansel and Gretel*, scarier than any witch in any story I had ever read, my mom ran to the front edge of the stage and began shouting at the sixth graders seated on the floor in front of her.

"So you think it's funny when someone has an accident, do you? So you think it's funny when someone gets hurt?"

She held out her hand. Blood was running down her arm from one of the slippery, broken pieces of glass from the shattered bowl.

"Emily, it's all right," Mr. Stuart said to her in a low, steady voice. "Let's get your hand cleaned up."

"It is not all right!" She whirled back to face the sixth graders. "I hope you're ashamed of yourselves! I hope your parents are ashamed of you, too!"

I didn't wait to see what would happen next. I slipped down from the stage and found Carly cowering all alone in her front-row seat.

"Let's go."

Clutching her pink jacket, Carly followed me out to the lobby, where the tables were still laden with leftover intermission snacks. At first I was relieved that she wasn't crying, but her face was so pale, greenish white, that I was afraid she might get sick instead.

"She got so mad," Carly whispered. "First she was laughing, and everything was funny, and then she got so mad. And her hand—Cooper, it was all bleeding."

"It'll be okay," I said. But nothing was going to be okay. "She ruined it," I burst out. I wanted to add, *She ruins everything.* But I couldn't say that to Carly.

"What's going to happen with the rest of the show?" Carly asked. "Will they still do the judging?"

Who cared?

"I don't know," I said.

I led Carly to the steps up to the second floor of the school. We sat down in the shadows, waiting in silence. I tried to think of an alphabet game to play to pass the time. The three of us used to love alphabet games, making endless alphabetical lists of countries, foods, animals, flowers. Now we could have an alphabet game of disaster: A for anger; B for broken bowl; C for chicken, or maybe C for catastrophe.

From inside the auditorium came a roar of applause. The judges must have delivered their verdict. Mr. Pasta had to have won: how could the parent team win with their dessert unfinished and half of it lying on the auditorium floor?

People began filing out. I wished Mom would show up quickly, so we could go home before I saw anybody I knew. I didn't even want to see Spencer or Ben; most of all, I didn't want to see Lindsay. How could I face Lindsay ever again, after she had been right there on the stage, seeing it all at close range?

"There she is. There's Mom." I left my hiding place on the stairs and gave her an urgent wave. She crossed the room to meet us.

I wasn't sure how I expected her to act—still angry? Ashamed? Plunged back into depression? What I didn't expect was her wide smile and torrent of words.

"We were robbed!" She laughed loudly. "Every single judge voted for your Mr. Pasta! Talk about rigged. Mousse is so last year. People are moussed out. Moussed up!" She exploded into laughter again. Over her spasm of giggles she could hardly get the next word out. "Mousstified!"

She was still laughing as we trailed behind her to the car.

That night I woke up abruptly in the darkness. I could hear music playing on the stereo downstairs: a driving bluegrass fiddle CD Mom liked to play to pump herself up when she was working. The clock on my nightstand read 3:15. I didn't know if she was up late, or up early, or was never going to go to bed at all. She didn't really have a choice: it was the night before Carly's play—no, the morning of Carly's play. I measured the time in my head: the play was going to begin at 7 p.m., in a little less than sixteen hours.

Thirsty now, I crept down the hall to the bathroom and gulped a glass of water. Then I stole soundlessly to the top of the stairs and peered down from the dimness of the landing to the glaring brightness of the living room. In the few moments that it took my eyes to adjust to the light, I willed the gingerbread house to be finished, every candy decoration painted, ready to be nibbled on by a hungry Hansel and Gretel. But it wasn't.

The house looked the same as it had before I left for "Pasta Live," painted in meticulous detail on the left side of the door while the right side stood bare. A heap of wire coat hangers, intended to form the bars of

Hansel's cage, covered the couch. No progress at all had been made on the oven.

Go back to bed, I told myself.

I tiptoed downstairs and through the living room, past the abandoned dining room table buried under bolts of fabric and flyers printed up for the art show at the Community Table. Mom was sitting on the yellow-stained kitchen floor, with all the contents from the pantry cupboard spread out around her.

She whirled her head around. "Cooper! You startled me!"

I flinched, startled myself, afraid of what she would say next.

But she was smiling. "We have lived in this house for ten years!" she exclaimed. "Ten *years*! And this is the first time anyone has thoroughly cleaned and organized this pantry. Look at this stuff!" She gestured to half a dozen cereal boxes. "Doesn't anyone in this family ever throw away a cereal box once it's empty? You'd think we were maintaining a cereal box museum. And talk about crumbs! Why we haven't had a whole civilization of mice established here I'll never know."

For the first time she seemed to remember that it was three in the morning. Her face softened with concern. "What is it, Coopster? Did you have a bad dream? Do you feel sick?"

"I couldn't sleep."

"I can make you some warm milk. Are you hungry? How about a bowl of cereal? But don't touch any of these! They're all too old. I'm going to make a spread-sheet on the computer for our cereal inventory. Every time we buy a new box, I'll enter it on the spreadsheet, with its expiration date, and once a month I'll go through the pantry and toss any old boxes that aren't fit to eat. I'm going to put a sticker on each box when it comes in. Every month will have a different color. Then it will be easy for all of us to keep track of the dates. So far I've done blue for September, and red for October, and yellow for November."

Sure enough, I saw a row of stickered cereal boxes lined up on the floor in front of the oven door.

"I'm not hungry," I said. "I was thirsty, so I got a drink of water, and I heard the music playing, so I came downstairs to see what was going on."

"What's going on," my mother said, raising her voice exultantly over the crescendo of the fiddle music, "is that this family is finally getting *organized*!"

I looked again at the five cereal boxes, two with red stickers, one with a blue sticker, and two with yellow stickers. Beneath my thin pajama top, my heart pounded as if I had sprinted around the middle school track.

I'm scared, I wanted to cry, and then maybe she would hold me on her lap and hug me as if I was little like Carly. But I couldn't.

Because what I was scared of was *her.*

16

At breakfast, Mom was as exuberant as she had been at three in the morning. The contents of the pantry cupboard remained spread out over the kitchen floor.

"Don't say it!" she warned Carly, in a teasing tone. "'The house isn't finished, the cage isn't finished, where is the oven?' The play isn't until seven tonight. It's only seven a.m. now. I have twelve more hours!"

"Mrs. Brattle keeps asking about it. She wants us to be able to practice with the real cage and real oven. Right now we're just using a chair for the cage and a big cardboard box for the oven, and pretending they're real."

"Pretending is good for the imagination." Mom's voice had become less lilting. "Look, if the school is going to rely on the volunteer efforts of busy working moms who have a thousand other things to do, they have to be willing to be flexible. They can't expect us to drop everything else in our lives, can they?"

No, I thought, *they can't expect you to postpone an important job like labeling all the cereal boxes in the pantry.*

Her face brightened again. "Don't worry, honey. I'm not going to let you down, I promise."

"I know," Carly said. It hurt my heart how much Carly still seemed to believe her.

To my surprise and relief, nobody at school said anything about my mother, except for one kid in the Food Fun class who called over to me, "Your mother's weird!" Ben silenced the kid with a look.

Instead of cooking that day, we ate the leftover intermission snacks while Mr. Pasta praised our performance at "Pasta Live." I had been afraid that we would watch the videotape of the show. We didn't, but then I worried that maybe we didn't watch it just because of the awful half that had my mother in it.

Lindsay came over to me after the bell rang. "Were you nervous?" she asked.

I didn't know what she meant: nervous being onstage with Mom, wondering what crazy thing she would do next?

"Being onstage, doing the helping?" she continued. "I was sure I'd mess up, and Mr. Pasta would lose, and it would be my fault."

"Well, your team didn't lose. Our team lost." I knew I sounded like a poor sport.

"Of course your team lost! Nobody can beat Mr. Pasta's cooking," Lindsay said consolingly. "That's why if I *had* messed up, and he *had* lost, I would have felt so guilty."

"Well, you didn't," I said again. I turned away and

hurried to my next class, sick inside at how I had acted, but it was all for the best in the end: Lindsay wasn't going to be able to go on liking someone with a mother who was that weird.

Thinking about Mom's hideous scene at "Pasta Live" was bad; thinking about the unfinished set for Carly's play was worse. Maybe *I* could make a halfway decent cage out of the wire hangers. I wished I could get Ben and Spencer to come over after school to help, but I was too ashamed: ashamed of what our house looked like, ashamed of my mom, ashamed of what had happened at "Pasta Live," ashamed of myself for having let it happen.

When the bell rang at the end of eighth-period social studies, Mr. Stuart stopped by my desk.

"Hey, Coop," he said.

I hurriedly stuffed my binder into my backpack.

"I just wanted to make sure your mother was doing all right."

"You mean her hand?" But I knew that wasn't all that Mr. Stuart meant. "Sure, it's fine. It's all good."

"Cooper, if you ever need to talk, remember that I'm here."

But I had already shrugged on my backpack and headed out the door.

When I arrived home at three-thirty, the first thing I saw was my mother, pliers in hand, putting the final touches on a cleverly constructed wire cage standing in the middle of the living room. The oven—a large, papier-mâché dome painted to look like bricks—was finished, too. The gingerbread house was still only half painted, but I could take care of that in an hour or two. The candy decorations didn't have to be perfect, whatever Michelangelo's views would have been on the subject. They just had to be done.

By five o'clock the house was completed. I felt giddy with relief. I remembered the best line from "Jabberwocky": "O frabjous day! Callooh! Callay!" The whole world was bursting with glorious frabjousness.

"We have to be at school by six-fifteen to get our costumes on," Carly announced. "What if I forget my lines? What if I can't remember a single word?"

"Won't there be a prompter?" I asked. "Someone standing offstage who can read you the lines if you forget them? Besides, you won't forget them. You've only practiced them forty-three million times."

Mom was going to drop us off in the station wagon with the gingerbread house and then return to get the oven and the cage.

"I'll see you in ten minutes," she said, as we stood by the side door of the school with the sections of the gingerbread house lying on the ground beside us. "I need to swing by the Community Table to drop off these flyers for the art show, and then I'll head back home for the oven and cage. Don't worry, I can get them into the car on my own. Break a leg, my darling Gretel!"

Carly looked bewildered.

"It means 'good luck,'" I told her. "Theater people always say it. Why, I don't know."

A couple of arriving dads helped me carry the gingerbread house into the gym. Carly danced off to get dressed in her Gretel costume. Once the house was set up on the stage, I chose two seats in the third row of folding chairs, one for me and one for my mom.

Carly's teacher, who had been my teacher, too, tapped me on the shoulder. "The house is beautiful!" she gushed. "Your mother is so creative! I have to say I was getting a bit frantic this last day or two: I don't like to cut things this close. But this house was definitely worth the wait."

I forced a smile. "Mom usually comes through."

I hoped it was true. Everything had changed so much in the last few months that I didn't know what *usually* meant for my mother anymore.

"Where *is* your mom?" Mrs. Brattle asked. "Is she getting the oven and cage from the car? I can send some kids out to help her."

"No, she had to run one quick errand. She'll be here any minute."

Mrs. Brattle looked at her watch. I looked at mine, too: 6:40.

The teacher turned away and bustled off to help one of the birds who had misplaced her beak. I alternated between looking at my watch—6:41, 6:42, 6:43—and twisting around in my seat to see if my mom was coming through the back doors of the gym.

Maybe I should wait for her in the parking lot? I left my jacket spread out over the two chairs to hold our place.

Car after car pulled into the parking lot, but not our station wagon. Finally, when my watch said 6:59, I abandoned my post and hurried back to my seat. I couldn't miss Carly's grand entrance, when she would utter the first line of the entire play. Anxiety churned in my stomach. What would they use as a cage for Hansel? Or an oven for the wicked witch?

At ten past seven, Mom still hadn't arrived—unless she had come in a different door? And carried the missing set pieces backstage?

The lights in the gym were turned off, and Mrs. Brattle came forward to welcome the audience. Her speech seemed longer than it needed to be, as if she were trying to stall for time.

At last the play began. Carly walked up the steps to the stage with the second grader who was playing Hansel. They stood together in front of the closed curtain: Carly had told me that the curtain wouldn't go up to reveal the gingerbread house until later on.

"Hansel, I'm hungry!"

"Poor Father has no food for us to eat."

I hardly listened. How long could it possibly take someone to drop off some flyers at a building not half a mile away? Of course, Mom also had to go home and pick up the cage and oven. But still.

Hansel and Gretel wandered through the make-believe woods, accompanied by a parade of twittering birds and furry woodland animals. Exhausted, they fell asleep.

Then the curtain rose. A murmur of appreciation ran through the audience. The gingerbread house did look perfect, like a house for a play on Broadway, a house that would have done Michelangelo proud. One glance told me that the oven and cage still weren't there.

Hansel and Gretel woke up and exclaimed over the gingerbread house with delight. Cautiously they began taking small pretend bites out of one of the chocolate-colored shutters.

"Nibble, nibble, little mousie. Who's that nibbling at my housie?" cried Jodie, the witch, who looked about as terrifying as a second grader could be.

It came time for the witch to put Hansel into the cage. Mrs. Brattle darted onto the stage, carrying a tall chair with a back made of wooden rungs. It must have been the chair they had used in rehearsal. Crouched behind the chair, Hansel could poke his finger through the rungs so that the witch could feel how well he was fattening.

But a chair didn't really look anything like a cage.

From the other side of the stage, Mrs. Brattle shoved out a large cardboard carton. The front-facing side had a cutout door, fastened on with duct tape.

But a cardboard carton didn't really look anything like an oven.

With a coaxing smile, the witch tried to get Gretel to test the heat of the oven. Gretel pretended not to know how to do it.

"Please show me, kind mother."

Impatient, the witch yanked open the cardboard door. Gretel pounced. With all her might she shoved the witch inside.

Thud! The carton crashed over backward. Unseen, the witch emitted one horrified wail.

Gales of laughter erupted from the audience. Behind his chair cage, even Hansel was convulsed with giggles. The only two people who weren't laughing were me and Carly, who had frozen in place, as if overcome by the destruction she had wrought.

Mrs. Brattle rushed onstage to see if Jodie was all right. The audience applauded when Jodie emerged from the carton, evidently unharmed. Jodie gave them a shaky wave.

What would happen now? The story couldn't end with the witch leaping out of the oven to be comforted by her teacher and cheered by the crowd.

After a whispered conference with Mrs. Brattle, the witch stepped back inside the oven. The teacher closed the makeshift oven door and retreated out of sight. Now Gretel could free Hansel from his chair cage, take the witch's treasure, and head back to the woodcutter's cottage.

I waited for Carly to say her line: "Hansel, the witch is dead! Now we can go home to Father!"

No words came out of Carly's mouth.

I strained my ears to hear if the offstage prompter would whisper the line. The silence stretched on. Finally, Hansel himself hissed to her, "Hansel, the witch is dead!"

The man sitting behind me chuckled. I hadn't known I could hate anyone the way I hated him.

Carly opened her mouth. "Hansel—"

Her face crumpled, and she ran offstage.

That was the end of the play. Mrs. Brattle came onstage and in a narrator's voice gave the conclusion of the story: Hansel and Gretel's reunion with their father, news of the death of their wicked stepmother, and "They all lived happily ever after." The actors came out for their bows, first the birds and the forest animals, then the father and stepmother, then Jodie as the witch, and then, all by himself, Hansel. Gretel never appeared.

Someone from the audience called out, "Gretel!" A few other parents took up the chant, but Mrs. Brattle silenced them with a wave of her hand. After one last round of applause for the entire cast, the curtain came down.

I ran up the steps by the side of the stage and behind the heavy purple velvet curtain. Mrs. Brattle had her arm around Carly, who was crying as if her heart would break. Jodie hovered next to them, together with a few somber, stricken birds.

When Carly saw me, she broke free of Mrs. Brattle and ran into my embrace. "Oh, Cooper!" She buried her face in my shirt.

At that moment, my mom pushed her way through the curtain, carrying the wire cage.

"You're too late," I announced. "In case you haven't noticed, the play is over."

She had looked distraught, out of breath, her hair disheveled, but at my hostile tone, she drew herself up-right.

"And you've never been late for anything, I suppose? Cooper, I was up all night working, and most of the night before that. When I left the Community Table, I was so exhausted I was starting to fall asleep at the wheel, so I pulled over and took a nap for just a few minutes. Is that a crime?"

"Look at Carly!" The harsh, angry voice didn't feel like my own. "She's crying."

"And it's all my fault?" Mom demanded.

I didn't reply.

She turned and marched back out of the gym, still lugging the wire-hanger cage. I had no choice but to grab Carly's hand and hurry after her.

I hated her even more than I hated the man who had laughed when Carly forgot her line. It *was* a crime to have ruined Carly's play, and I would never forgive her for it as long as I lived.

17

After school the next day, I finished my homework right away—all I had was math—and went to Carly's room. She had the Inchland deeds—Gran-Dan's deeds for the eight square inches of the Yukon—spread out on her table, next to her stack of Inchland drawings and Inchitella and Parsley's furnished stable.

I sat down next to her. "You took the deeds out of your treasure box."

"I wanted to look at them. *You* look at them, Cooper. It doesn't say anywhere on them that they're only good for a little while, does it?"

"You mean do they have an expiration date? Like coupons at the grocery store?"

Once upon a time my mom had gone grocery shopping every week with a sheaf of coupons clipped from the Sunday newspaper advertising circulars, and Carly and I had helped her find the coupon items. It had made grocery shopping feel like a treasure hunt.

"Uh-huh."

I picked up the deed that was closest to me on the table. It was bigger than I remembered it, maybe five inches by seven inches—bigger than the whole of the eight square inches of Inchland that Carly and I owned put together. "Deed of Land," it said on the top, with fancy gold curlicues around the edges. I skimmed the long paragraphs of legal language on both sides of the deed: "Witnesseth that . . ." "this conveyance and everything herein contained shall be wholly subject to a perpetual easement for ingress and egress, to, from, over and upon the tract herein conveyed for the use of the owner . . ."

Perpetual sounded like forever. There was a seal at the bottom of the back side of the deed, from the Klondike Big Inch Land Co. Inc.

"I think it's still good," I told Carly.

"Cooper, what if we went there?"

"To Canada? For our winter vacation?"

"No. Not with Mom. Just us."

There was no point in asking her how she expected to get there, whether she thought we could walk a thousand miles, or however far it was to the Yukon, or whether she thought Mom would be as indifferent to our absence as Inchitella's parents were to hers. Or what she thought we'd find when we got there—the real castle, the real stable, the real flying rabbit.

"I wish we could," I said.

"Maybe Gran-Dan would take us. He must want to go there, too."

"No," I said. "Gran-Dan didn't want his deeds anymore. That's why he gave them to us. To get rid of them."

Besides, Inchland was just more artsiness, for bums who didn't want to work and crazy moms who didn't do what they were supposed to do to take care of their kids.

"We'll never get rid of our deeds, will we, Cooper?"

"No."

"We'll keep them forever and ever, won't we? And we'll go there someday?"

"Sure," I said. There was no harm in pretending. "We'll go there someday."

That Saturday morning I slept late and didn't bother waking up for Gran-Dan's phone call.

The morning was cold. Shards of frost lay littered on the lawn like broken glass. Once I'd roused myself from bed and gobbled down a bowl of cereal for breakfast, I found Carly in her room, seated at the little table by her window.

"Where's Mom?" I asked.

"She's asleep."

She hadn't slept late for months. Wild hope stirred in my chest. Instantly I tried to douse my joy with guilt. I shouldn't be rooting for a return of her long months of sadness, when she lay in a darkened room all day long, not caring about anything.

"She said she was tired," Carly added.

The geyser of hope inside me gurgled again. I dropped into the little chair across from Carly.

"You need to get a bigger chair," I told her. "For when normal-size people come to visit."

"Oh, Cooper." Carly gave the first smile I had seen since the night of the play. Maybe she was grateful, too, that our mom was still sleeping. "You're normal-size for a sixth grader, and I'm normal-size for a second grader. And Inchitella and Parsley are normal-size for Inchies."

"How *are* Inchitella and Parsley?" I could see the Inchland deeds still spread out on the table.

"They're fine." She paused. "I was wondering if maybe we *could* make them be grownups, so that they *could* get married."

"Sure. What about Button? Is she older, too?"

"I don't think she gets older. Because she's magic. Regular people get older, but flying bunnies always stay the same age."

"Sounds good to me."

"If they grow up, and if they get married, they could have a baby. A teensy-tiny, itty-bitty baby," Carly suggested.

"Boy or girl?"

Carly looked up at the ceiling, the way she sometimes did when she was thinking hard about something.

"Both. Teeny-tiny, itty-bitty Inchie twins. And we can go see them when we visit Inchland. Do you think they'll know who we are? When we get there?"

"Maybe," I said, not really paying attention to the question. I was listening to see if I heard any sound from Mom's room, any sign that she was awake and stirring. The longer she slept, the better it was for all of us.

I spent the afternoon at Ben's house, working with Ben and Spencer on a science project, leaving Carly at home with Mom. We had to design a racing car powered by a mousetrap. The goal was to see how far it would go and how fast it would go. Actually, the first goal was to see if it would go at all.

After two hours, our car shot across Ben's gleaming living room floor at dazzling speed, and Ben's mom had decided that the finger Spencer caught in the mousetrap on one of our early tries wasn't broken, just bruised and battered. She gave him a bag of frozen peas to hold against it to keep the swelling down.

"Do you think mousetraps are cruel and unusual punishment for mice?" Spencer asked, gazing down at his wounded hand lying flattened under a pound of frozen peas.

"No," Ben said. "The mouse is killed instantly. It doesn't feel anything."

"My finger feels something," Spencer said mournfully. "I think mousetraps are cruel and unusual punishment for fingers."

Spencer and I walked home from Ben's together. My house was halfway in between Ben's house and Spencer's house, the way my family used to be halfway in between the order and calm of Ben's house and the noisy mess of Spencer's. Now my family belonged on Mars.

We were mostly silent on the way. Spencer kicked a stone but didn't bother pretending that he was scoring the winning goal in the finals for the World Cup. Despite all Spencer's joking, his finger must really hurt.

"Ben's lucky," I said as we neared my yard.

"Why?"

Didn't Spencer know? "Because his house is perfect, and his parents are perfect, and he's perfect."

"Are you implying that I'm not perfect?" Spencer asked with mock indignation.

"You know what I mean."

"Maybe it's boring being perfect," Spencer said.

"Does Ben look bored to you?"

"No," Spencer admitted.

We reached my house; although the dusk was deepening, all the lights were turned off. I hoped Carly was out with Mom, and not cowering there in the semi-darkness.

"Hey," Spencer said in a low voice. "Don't look now, but somebody is coming."

Despite Spencer's warning, I whirled around. Lindsay and her friend Allison were walking toward us.

"Hi!" Allison called to us.

"Hi!" Spencer said back.

Lindsay didn't say anything.

I didn't say anything.

"We're out for a walk," Allison said, as the two girls approached where we were standing.

"So are we," Spencer said. "We were working on our mousetrap car, at Ben's house."

"Wow!" Allison said. "We were working on *our* mousetrap car, at Tamara's house!"

"This is Cooper's house," Spencer said, pointing to it.

"It is?" Allison asked, as if stunned by the news. Lindsay was staring very hard at the ground.

"Wow," Allison went on. "We didn't know you lived here. I mean, Lindsay didn't know that Cooper lived here. I mean, we both thought somebody else lived here. We were just walking by. You know, on our way home from Tamara's house. Where we were working on our mousetrap car. The way you were working on your mousetrap car."

Lindsay finally looked up and gave me a quick, sheepish smile.

"Did your mousetrap car turn out okay?" she asked. It was obvious that she was speaking to me, not to Spencer.

"Yeah," I said.

"Except that I caught my finger in the mousetrap, and now I may have to have it amputated," Spencer added.

Both girls laughed.

I tried to think of something funny of my own to say, but I couldn't. But maybe it didn't matter. Ben was perfect, and Spencer was funny, but it was obvious that

Lindsay liked me, not Ben, not Spencer. And she liked me even after "Pasta Live," even though my mother was weird and their mothers were normal.

"Well, I guess we'd better go," Lindsay said.

"Sure," I said. I gave Lindsay a huge smile, and she gave me a huge smile back.

Reluctantly, I headed up the path toward home.

"If I die from the amputation, you can have my iPod," Spencer called after me.

"You goof," I called back, turning around to smile at Lindsay one last time.

I had been afraid I'd find Carly huddled on the couch again, hidden under a blanket. But the house seemed to be completely empty. Mom must be out somewhere. I hoped Carly was with her, unless she was playing at Jodie's house; but Jodie's house was dark, too.

Just to be sure, I checked Carly's room; she wasn't there. Relieved, I went into my own room, but as I was about to sprawl on my bed, I saw it: a sheet of paper left prominently on my pillow, where I wouldn't be able to miss it.

In Carly's big second-grade printing, all in caps, I read:

DEER COOPER
I HAV GONE TO INCHLAND
LOVE CARLY

18

Don't panic! I told myself sternly. I took a few slow, deep breaths to calm my racing heart.

Carly was only seven. She couldn't have gone very far. I had last seen her before I left for Ben's, around one o'clock. Mom had still been home then. It was five-thirty now. I didn't know exactly when she had left the note on my pillow, but it might have been just an hour ago, or even less. How far could a little girl walk in an hour? Of course, depending on when Mom had left, it might be a whole lot longer.

Which way would she have headed? Inchland was in the frozen Yukon, so north. But would Carly know which direction was north? Was that something a second grader would know?

For lack of a better idea, I threw on my jacket, hurried outside, and started walking north. The mountains were on the west, so north was always the direction with the mountains on your left. I tried to think of what Carly would be wearing. I should have checked the closet before I left the house to see which of her coats was missing—probably the pink one. Pink was Carly's favorite color, and she'd want to look her prettiest to meet Parsley and Inchitella.

The thought made my heart swell with Inchitella's frozen, diamond tears.

As I walked, I looked to the right and to the left for a glimpse of pink. "Carly!" I called, just in case she had stopped to rest somewhere out of view. "Carly!" My voice sounded desperate and pathetic, calling for someone who might already be miles away, or might even just be at a friend's house, pretending the friend's house was Inchland. I tried to remember all of Carly's favorite places for make-believe: the overgrown bushes at the edge of the Deer Creek Elementary field, the "castle" at the park built of plywood and old rubber tires, the tree house at the home of one of her other friends—what was her name? Katie, maybe. I should have looked all those places first; I should have started with the places where Carly might pretend to find Inchland.

Breaking into a jog, I trotted back home. The lights shining through the living room window sent my heart soaring, but then I remembered I had left them on when I went out. Still, I gave one quick check inside to see if Carly had by chance returned home before setting out again. This time, I'd be more systematic. I'd make a mental list of every possible place she could be, check each place, and then cross it off the list, starting with the places closest to home, and radiating out from there.

I'd start with the school, the park, and Katie's tree house.

At Deer Creek Elementary, my eyes searched the playground. It was hard to believe that I had been a student there just a few short months ago; I felt like I had been a middle schooler forever. There on the playground were the monkey bars where Ben and Spencer and I had loved to climb all through third grade: Ben with effortless strength and grace, Spencer always cracking us up as he was about to fall off, me watching the others, taking it all in, drawing a picture of the three of us on the monkey bars that got a blue ribbon at the school art show.

I didn't see any flashes of pink anywhere, but it was getting too dark to see.

"Carly!"

I jogged up to the fringe of bushes at the far end of the school field. This had always been one of my own places to hide and dream. During fourth grade, Ben and Spencer had started hanging around with another kid, Matt P., and for a while I had thought they liked Matt P. better than they liked me, and I would slink off to sulk in the bushes and make up stories about a band of three pirates named Ben, Spencer, and Cooper, and how they made a fourth pirate named Matt P. walk the plank.

Carly wasn't there hiding in the bushes.

The park was also deserted—who would go to a park after dark in December? Well, maybe a little girl who was running away to Inchland, but Carly wasn't there. On the base of the slide, I found one toddler-size shoe. How could somebody lose a shoe? Wouldn't you notice it was gone as soon as you started walking?

At Katie's house, light poured from the windows into the yard. Afraid they would think I was a trespasser, I darted over to the tree in the backyard and swung myself easily up the rope ladder to the wooden platform, but I knew already that Carly wasn't there.

My cheeks stung from the frosty air, and my fingers inside my gloves were cramped with cold. Maybe Carly had given up and returned home. Summoning hope, I ran back toward my house. She must be there by now, and if she wasn't, I'd call Ben and Spencer and they could help me look, each of us taking a different direction: north, south, east. I would just have to hope that Carly hadn't headed west instead.

Just as I burst, panting, into the still silent house, calling Carly's name one last hoarse time, I heard my mother's key opening the door into the kitchen from the garage.

Please, please, please, let Carly be with her.

Mom stumbled into the kitchen, carrying two overstuffed shopping bags; the bottom had given way on one of them, and she was struggling to hold on to it from underneath. There was no sign of Carly.

"Cooper, quick, take this bag before I drop it," she ordered.

"Carly's gone," I told her. "She's run away."

"What do you mean, she's run away?"

The bottom of the shopping bag gave one final rip, and everything in it cascaded onto the filthy, littered kitchen floor. Christmas presents, I saw: flat boxes that would be board games; thicker boxes that would be jigsaw puzzles; a large doll, dressed in an old-fashioned costume, with a fur-trimmed coat and hat and muff, staring up at us with glassy, unseeing eyes.

"Look what you did!" my mother yelled.

"Look what *I* did?" Now the fear had turned to rage. "Mom, Carly is gone. She left a note. She's run away. To Inchland."

"Inchland?"

How many times did I have to explain it to her? "Gran-Dan's deeds? To the Yukon? Our imaginary country?"

I wanted to shake her, to say something that would make her turn back into the person she had been before.

"Why aren't you out looking for her?" she demanded.

"I've been looking for her! What do you think I've been doing for the last hour? I came home to see if maybe she had come back while I was out searching, or to call Ben and Spencer and get them to help, or to call the police."

The word *police* seemed to energize her. "All right, Cooper, you go back outside and look for her on foot, and I'll search in the car."

I imagined myself wearily circling again around the school, the park, Katie's tree house, still calling Carly's name, still finding nothing. What else could I do?

The doorbell rang, a sudden, sharp explosion of sound. My mother and I both ran to answer it. I got there first.

It was Jodie's dad, and clinging to his hand was Carly.

"Look what I found!" he said. "I was driving along when I saw a familiar-looking little girl walking by herself down the street, and I said, Wait, isn't that Carly? And sure enough it was. She tried to tell me something about where she was going, but I couldn't quite make it out. But here she is now, safe and sound."

"Josh, thank you," my mom said smoothly, as if seven-year-olds normally wandered around town after dark all by themselves and were given rides home again by various dads who just happened to be driving by on their errands. What if Jodie's dad hadn't seen Carly? How long would she have wandered in the dark all by herself?

"No problem," Jodie's dad said.

As soon as he left, I hugged Carly so tight I was half afraid I'd smother her.

"Cooper, stop! Cooper, I have to go to the bathroom!"

I released her, and she raced upstairs.

I turned to face my mother. "Mom. What if Jodie's dad hadn't found Carly? It could have been hours before anybody found her. You left her alone, *again*, and went off—shopping!"

"Shopping isn't a crime, Cooper," she said with exaggerated patience. "You sound like your grandfather."

Her words seemed logical enough, but there was nothing logical about leaving a seven-year-old home by herself, or ruining Carly's play, or making a scene during "Pasta Live," or not paying the electricity bill, or organizing all the cereal boxes in the pantry at three in the morning.

I had to tell her. Even if she hadn't listened to Jodie's mom, I had to make her listen to me.

"Mom, there's something wrong with you. You need to go back to the doctor. You need to be taking your medication."

She gave a snort of bitter laughter. "And where did you get your medical degree?"

"Mom, other people can see it, too. On Thanksgiving —I could hear you talking with Jodie's mom—"

I broke off as her face twisted with fury. She raised her hand, as if about to slap me full in the face, my mother who had never once struck me or Carly.

I backed away from her, frightened not by the possible blow but by the anger, even the hatred, that shone from her blazing eyes.

As I started up the stairs, she followed, shouting.

"So you think I'm mentally ill? So you think it's my fault that Carly ran away? Who filled Carly's head with nonsense about Inchland? Who made Carly think it was a real place she could go to? I'm asking you a question, Cooper! Answer me, Cooper!"

The next thing I knew she was in Carly's room, where Carly, still wearing her pink jacket, was curled into a tight little pink ball on the bed. I leaped to get to the table ahead of Mom, but she was already striding across the room toward it.

Her frenzied fury fell on Inchitella and Parsley's tiny stable.

With one outthrust arm, she knocked it off the table to the floor, then stomped on it with her heavy shoe, splintering the stable to pieces.

"Look at these!" She snatched up the eight precious deeds that had been hidden so carefully in Carly's treasure box. "One square inch of the Yukon!" she shouted. "One square inch of *nothing*!"

She ripped the deeds in half, then in half again, and in half again, and tossed the torn pieces into the air.

Then, she caught herself with a shuddering sob, as if overcome by what she had just done, and fled from the room.

The ragged scraps of the deeds covered the floor, half burying the ruins of the stable: the final snowstorm fallen over Inchland.

19

She left the house. I heard the car gunning out of the driveway.

Carly lay utterly still—not crying, not speaking, not moving.

"Come on," I said, getting up from the table. "We have to get out of here before she comes back."

My sister didn't reply. I took her hand and pulled her up, too. A few scraps of the Inchland deeds fell from her lap to the littered floor.

Carly stooped to retrieve them. "We can tape them back together."

"No," I said. "We can't."

It was dark at Jodie's house, so Carly and I walked the five blocks to Spencer's house. Spencer's mother opened the door when we rang the bell.

"Why, Cooper, Carly, what is it?"

I had to say it out loud. I didn't know if I could.

"My mother."

"What's happened? Is she hurt?"

I shook my head. "I think she's mentally ill."

Her face turned from puzzlement to pained understanding. "When I saw her at the cooking program, something didn't seem right, but I thought it was just the stress of being up there onstage, and the accident. And then when I saw her at the grocery store a few days later, she seemed perfectly fine. Spencer hasn't said anything— Oh, Cooper, I wish I had known."

Safe now, with a normal, caring grownup in charge, Carly burst into tears and let Spencer's mother fold her into a hug. I felt nothing. But I was thinking plenty.

"I need to call my grandfather. In New Jersey. But I don't have his phone number."

I had never called him; he always called us.

Spencer's mom called information and got the number for me, writing it down on a scrap of paper. "Tell him you and Carly can stay here as long as you want," she told me. She handed me the phone and led me to the privacy of Spencer's room, beckoning Spencer to come out with her into the hall.

"Hey, dude—" Spencer began, his face lighting up at the unexpected sight of me in his doorway. "Good news: the doctor thinks my finger can be saved up to the knuckle."

I tried to smile.

"Not now, Spencey," Spencer's mom said. "Cooper needs to use the phone."

The two of them left me alone, shutting the door behind them as they went.

The phone rang so many times that I was afraid Gran-Dan wasn't home, but finally he answered. "Hello?"

"Gran-Dan—" I stopped, unable to go on. It had been hard enough to say it to Spencer's mom. How could I say it to Gran-Dan?

"Cooper? What is it?"

"Mom—"

"What happened? Is Carly all right?"

I knew he'd care most about Carly.

"Cooper, is everything okay?"

No, nothing was okay, and it wasn't going to be okay ever again.

"Mom wrecked Inchland."

"Inchland?"

"She smashed the stable and ripped up the deeds."

I knew my grandfather had no idea what I was talking about. I tried to explain, but it all came out in a jumble.

"Remember how she was so sad last summer? Well, she went to a doctor, to a psychiatrist, and she started taking medication, and it made her better for a while, but then I think she stopped taking it. And instead of being depressed, she was all hyper, and it got worse and worse, and she was horrible up onstage during 'Pasta Live,' and she didn't finish the set for Carly's play on time, and she fell asleep in the car, and ruined the play, and then Carly tried to run away to Inchland, just like Princess Inchitella ran away, and Mom said it was all my fault, and she wrecked Inchland."

"Where is she now?" Gran-Dan asked.

"Carly? She's here with me. We went to Spencer's."

"No. Emily. Your mother."

"I don't know. She left the house. She was crying. And driving really fast."

There was a long pause on the other end of the line. Then Gran-Dan said, "I can be there tomorrow. Let me speak to Spencer's mom, okay?"

I went to find her and handed her the phone. Then I went back to Spencer's room and climbed into Spencer's unmade bed and pulled the covers up. Spencer had Spider-Man sheets, and a Superman pillow, and an Iron Man comforter. I had never thought of Spencer as having a smell, but the bed smelled like Spencer. I liked how it smelled.

I planned to stay just where I was for a long, long time.

I slept in Spencer's room that night, in a borrowed sleeping bag on the floor. Carly slept on the couch in the family room. When Spencer and I woke up, around ten o'clock on Sunday morning, Carly was already awake and helping Spencer's mother make pancakes for everybody.

"Did my mom call?" I asked her. "While we were sleeping?"

"No, but I left her a message last night on your home phone, and on her cell phone, telling her that you're here."

In the afternoon, Spencer and I played video games,

while Carly and Spencer's mom worked on a thousand-piece jigsaw puzzle of Venice.

"It's probably more like a nine hundred fifty–piece puzzle," Spencer's mom apologized to Carly in advance. "With four boys and three dogs, puzzle pieces tend to vanish around here. But nine hundred fifty pieces should keep us pretty busy, don't you think?"

At five o'clock, just as Spencer and I were staggering up from the basement after four straight hours of playing Spencer's latest video game, the doorbell rang. My heart raced—what if it was my mom? But it wasn't my mom's voice I heard asking, "Are there any grandchildren of mine anywhere around here?"

It was Gran-Dan.

Carly hurled herself into his arms, and he scooped her up into the air. I let Gran-Dan hug me, too.

"Let's go," Gran-Dan said. He thanked Spencer's mom, and then we headed out to his rental car.

In the car, Carly asked, "Where's Mom?"

"We'll talk about everything when we get to your house," Gran-Dan said. So we drove in silence.

Gran-Dan hadn't been in the house yet; he didn't have a key. When we opened the front door and turned on the first light, I heard his sharp intake of breath. Sometimes I would try to tell myself that it wasn't so bad, that lots of people have messy houses, even Spencer has a messy house, but the way Gran-Dan caught his breath at the sight of it let me know I hadn't been making it up, it really was as bad as I thought it was.

"How long has it been like this?" he asked me.

"I don't know. A long time."

"Why didn't you tell me?" He sounded angry now, whether angry at Mom or angry at me, I didn't know. "Cooper, you're—what? Twelve years old?"

Eleven.

"You're old enough to know what's normal and what's not. Take a look at this place! Just look at it!"

I already knew what it looked like. I looked at it every day. I knew what the broken bowl at "Pasta Live" looked like, and the wooden chair–cage on the stage for Carly's play, and the wreckage of Inchland lying on the floor of Carly's room.

"I tried," I began.

"You tried," he said, his echo of my words obviously intended as a mockery.

"I did try!"

I wasn't sure that was even true. There were so many words that I had spoken inside my own head.

"Don't be mad at Cooper," Carly pleaded.

Gran-Dan looked down at her. Abruptly, he turned away for a moment; when he looked again at us, the anger had drained from his face. Instead, his eyes glistened.

"Cooper, I'm sorry. I didn't mean to blame you. And I don't blame your mother, either. This— It isn't anybody's fault."

Gran-Dan shoved a pile of the mess covering the couch onto the floor, with somewhat more force than necessary. "Come here, Carly." He pulled Carly onto his lap. I followed his example and shoved another pile of mess from the couch, so I could sit down next to the two of them.

"Okay," Gran-Dan said. "Where should we start?"

"Where's Mom?" Carly asked.

"I had to make some phone calls, but I found her. She's at the hospital. She's going to be there for a while."

"Did she have a car accident?" Carly asked. I had thought the same thing.

"No. She just needs some help from the doctors to get her moods more stable. Have you two ever heard of bipolar disorder? It's a mental illness where someone goes back and forth between a state of depression, like your mom was in last summer, and a state of mania, like she's been in this fall."

If that was what bipolar disorder was, it sure sounded like what Mom had.

"Your mom took medication for her depression, but then she went into a manic state, and she felt so good that she stopped taking the meds and never went back to the doctor for any more care."

So that was why the bottle of pills had disappeared.

"There is medicine she can take so she'll be more like her old self again," Gran-Dan went on, "but it will take some time."

"Will she die?" Carly asked.

"Nope. I think she's going to be okay." He sounded as if he was trying to convince himself as much as us.

"She tore up your deeds to Inchland," Carly said in a small voice. "She ripped them up into little pieces."

"That's what Cooper told me."

"We were going to try to go there, Cooper and me. For vacation, just the two of us. But then I couldn't wait, so I tried to go there all by myself."

Gran-Dan looked over at me. Was this another thing he was going to blame me for?

"It was Carly's idea," I said quickly. "I knew we couldn't really go there. I mean, it's so far, like a thousand miles away."

Carly glared at me. "You didn't say that, Cooper. You said you wanted to go."

"I said I wished we could go," I corrected her.

"Well, you know what?" Gran-Dan interrupted. "You two aren't the only ones who have wished you could go there. The Canadian government has had hundreds of inquiries over the years—thousands—from folks who wanted to go up there and see their land, find out which inch was theirs. But here's what they found out."

"There isn't any land?" I guessed.

"Oh, there's a piece of land, all right. The Quaker oats advertising man bought it for a thousand dollars, I think it was, back in the 1950s, and had all those deeds printed up. But the deeds were never registered in court, and then finally the Canadian government took the land away for nonpayment of property taxes."

"So it's not real," Carly said, as if checking to be sure she understood.

"Nope," Gran-Dan said. "It was just a real good way for someone to make money selling Quaker oats."

"It *was* real," I burst out. Sudden, shameful tears stung my eyes. "It was real to Carly and me."

Where were Inchitella and Parsley and Button going to live now that Mom had destroyed Inchland? Where could they go if there wasn't any Inchland at all, anywhere, and never had been?

"Look, Cooper, Carly." I could tell Gran-Dan was doing his best. "However you look at it, a square inch of land in Canada is awfully small and awfully far away. It wouldn't be much of a place to run to, even if the taxes had been paid, even if your mother hadn't ripped up the deeds."

"Is she really going to be okay?" I asked. "You need to tell us. We need to know."

There was a long silence. Then Gran-Dan said, "It depends." After another long pause, he went on. "Your mom will probably still have mood swings, high and low. But if she takes her medication, she should be pretty much like she was before."

I wasn't going to let him off so easily. "What if she doesn't? Take her medication?"

I have to give him credit: he looked straight into my eyes as he said, "I'm not going to lie to you, Cooper. If she doesn't take her medication, it probably won't be so good. So let's hope she does. I'm going to stay with you here in Colorado until things stabilize. And I can sell the house in Montclair and move out here if I have to."

Would it be a good or bad thing, having Gran-Dan live so close to us? Probably some of both. Either way, I was beginning to realize, there wasn't anything I could do about it.

Carly had fallen quiet for the last few minutes. Now she asked, "Is it snowing right now? In the Yukon? Where our square inch would be if we had it?"

"We *do* have it," I said. I waited for Gran-Dan to contradict me, tell me that a big kid like me should know better than to believe such foolishness, know better than to continue to lead a little kid like Carly astray. But he let me keep on talking.

"Carly, Inchland isn't up in the Yukon, or in the stuff we built in your room. It's inside you and inside me, and no one can rip it up or take it away."

"And it's snowing there right now?" she persisted. "With little diamond snowflakes?"

"Yes," I said softly. "It is."